The Gryphon Seal

Lost Tales of Kaphtu: Book One

By

Richard Purtill

authorHOUSE™

1663 LIBERTY DRIVE, SUITE 200
BLOOMINGTON, INDIANA 47403
(800) 839-8640
WWW.AUTHORHOUSE.COM

This book is a work of fiction. Places, events, and situations in this story are purely fictional and any resemblance to actual persons, living or dead, is coincidental.

© 2005 Richard Purtill.
All Rights Reserved.

No part of this book may be reproduced, stored in a retrieval system, or transmitted by any means without the written permission of the author.

First published by AuthorHouse 12/07/04

ISBN: 1-4208-0471-5 (sc)

Printed in the United States of America
Bloomington, Indiana

This book is printed on acid-free paper.

Other Books by Richard Purtill

The Golden Gryphon Feather
The Stolen Goddess
The Mirror of Helen
Enchantment at Delphi
The Parallel Man
Murdercon
J.R.R.Tolkien:
Myth, Morality, and Religion

This book is dedicated to my son,
Mark Purtill,
who suggested that I try my hand at a novel set in the
Edwardian period.
And, also to my friends
Lilia and Masha Castle
who love England and Greece
and enjoy my stories.

Cover painting by Suphontes

Thanks to:

Gord Wilson
Lucy Davis
Ron Bowles

For more about Lost Tales of Kaphtu,
The Kaphtu Trilogy, and other works
by Richard Purtill, visit our official
website at www.alivingdog.com

Chapter One

When I heard the steps outside the library door, I poised myself to hide the book I was reading in a drawer and pretend to be writing a shopping list I had on the table underneath the book. But I recognized Trephan's step and relaxed: he wouldn't betray me to Aunt Maddie even if his rather short-sighted eyes could recognize that the book I was reading was one I was not supposed to read. Trephan had been in the house when my mother was a girl: she, too, was a voracious reader and he rather liked to see me with a book in my hand. Aunt Maddie's maid, Solange, would have immediately tattled to Aunt Maddie and enjoyed getting me in trouble, and Aunt Ceal, though she might not have given me away, would have been very worried about me reading Mary Wolstonecroft's *Vindication of the Rights of Women*.

Trephan gave a knock at the door and opened it. He gave me his rather shy smile and said, "General Athlone and Miss Stone would like to see you in the sitting room, Miss Victoria ." I smiled back at him. "Thank you, Trephie," I said. "Do you have any idea of what it's all about?" He shook his head. "No, Miss Vicky" he said in a lower tone. "I've never known the General to come so unexpectedly, and your Aunt is very annoyed about something."

I followed him, feeling apprehensive, but rather pleased that Aunt Maddie was annoyed. She annoyed *me* often enough, and I didn't mind seeing her annoyed. Very ignoble Aunt Ceal would say: you shouldn't rejoice at the misfortunes of your enemies, but I was far from noble about Aunt Maddie. Of course Aunt Ceal would have been horrified if I had called Aunt Maddie an enemy, but in my eyes she was. She was always chipping away at my freedom, and my freedom was very important to me. Important enough to lie and steal for, and I resented that Aunt Maddie had made me a liar and a thief.

When Trephan ushered me into the sitting room, I looked with curiosity at General Athlone. He was our oldest living relative, and officially the head of the family. Much too often I had heard Aunt Maddie cite him as an authority for some of her more tiresome regulations. "General Athlone would be shocked to hear that one of his grandnieces was out without an escort...", or "...reading such a book...", or whatever my current sin (according to her) was. I didn't hold this against the General: I suspected that a tough old veteran of the Napoleanic Wars would be far less easily shocked than Aunt Maddie said, and she was simply using his name and authority as "head of the family" to reinforce her own wishes. Despite all of her talk about how men were superior to women, Aunt Maddie was quite fond of getting her own way with men, flattering and cajoling when she couldn't intimidate. With women, from poor Aunt Ceal to me and down to the maids, she expected instant obedience and no arguments.

The General, a fine looking man with old-fashioned side whiskers, looked at me with interest. "Well, you've grown quite a bit since I first saw you, Victoria" he said, "got a hint of your mother's red hair, too." Aunt Maddie pursed her lips. She thought that red hair was vulgar, and insisted that I wear a pomade on my hair to darken it and control its rebelliousness. The General coughed and said "I've some sad news for you; your Uncle Pettigrew has died, leaving your Aunt Margot all alone." "I'm very sorry to hear that," I told him quite sincerely. Uncle Pettigrew had been a professor of classics at Oxford and, in my view, added a certain amount of prestige to the family. Not in Aunt Maddie's view, of course; she regarded a university professor as somehow middle class. We were aristocracy, and could enter the church, the law, or the army (if you were a man, of course) but professions such as medicine and teaching were not for us.

"I've decided, as head of the family, that you should go and stay with your Aunt Margot. She was never very good at practical matters and she needs someone to cope with things for her. Your Aunt tells me that you're very good at helping out." Aunt Maddie may have put it that way to the General, but I had overheard her boast that I was as good as an extra maid in the house. "And your Aunt's eyesight is failing: she'd like someone to read to her. Your Aunt has told me that you have a good reading voice; says she sends you to read the Bible to some of her tenants. Not so sure that's a good idea. It was the late Queen's notion and I'm sure it does her credit, but one of my friends who has an estate in the Highlands sent his wife to read to their tenants and she came home with a flea in her ear: one of the tenants told her that she had her own Bible and could read it perfectly well herself."

I smiled at him and received a smile in return. General Athlone, far from being the ogre that Aunt

Maddie had depicted, was someone I could both admire and enjoy. Aunt Maddie's voice cut in, "I have told you, my dear General, that we cannot do without Victoria here: there are so many things she does for us. She goes to the bank for our weekly household expenses; there's no one else I could send..."

The General shook his head. "You've got lawyers; they'll send a clerk to collect the money and it's far safer than letting a young girl do it." Aunt Maddie pursed her lips again. A lawyer would charge a fee for such a service and Aunt Maddie hated parting with money. "No, the thing is, Maddie, that you're a selfish woman and always were. Margot can really use the girl and you can do without her. I'll send a carriage for her on Monday, and that's my final word. Now, if you'll leave us, I'd like to speak to Victoria privately."

Aunt Maddie hated to go, but she couldn't openly defy the head of the family. She swept out and the General regarded me sympathetically. "Sit down, Victoria. Vicky they'll call you I suppose. You've been on my conscience, girl. When your mother and father died so tragically and your Aunt Maddie offered to take you, it seemed the best solution. Should have probably sent you to Pettigrew and Margot then, but they couldn't really afford another mouth to feed. Pettigrew was just a don then, hadn't got his professorship. Now that I've finally got your father's affairs straightened out, you can get a small allowance from his estate. You can contribute to Margot's household expenses; she owns their old house in North Oxford. You won't mind that, will you, Vicky?"

"Oh, no," I said eagerly. "I wouldn't have liked contributing to expenses <u>here</u>, but I'd be glad to help Aunt Margot." He shook his head. "No need for you to help out here, from what our lawyers let slip. Maddie must be rich as Creosus. She'd have your money all right; hates spending and likes accumulating. She can't be an easy person to live with." I smiled at him. "It wasn't too bad, sir. Lots of the older servants remember my mother. I'll be sorry to leave them and poor Aunt Ceal."

He sighed. "I'm afraid that Celia is a lost case: her sister dominated her when they were children and now I don't think she could live without Maddie telling her what to do. You've had a thin time of it, Vicky, but I hope things will get better for you. Maybe meet a few young dons or undergraduates at Oxford and get yourself married. Not much chance of that in this house. And don't call me 'sir'; I'm not your officer. I'd be very pleased if you'd call me Uncle."

"This is really wonderful news for me, Uncle. Can I give you a niecely hug," I said impulsively. He held out his arms and we embraced. "Always did think your mother was the best of my brother's children" he said gruffly. "My Christian name's Sylvester, and most of my friends call me 'Vester'. Well, run along now. I'll have to read the riot act to Maddie to make sure you get out of here with no more argument." I slipped out the door hoping to avoid Aunt Maddie and saw Thomas, the coachman, waiting in the hall. "It's time for your visit to the Armatiges, Miss Vicky," he said. Actually, it was time for him to foregather at the public house with his cronies after dropping me at the Armitrage house, but this suited my plans very well. I'd just as soon be out of Aunt Maddie's orbit for a while until her rage at what had happened died down. "All right," I said. "Do you have my coat and hat?" he nodded. "Ivy brought them down." Ivy, one of the house-maids was one of my younger supporters in the house, while the housekeeper, Mrs. Varley, Solange, and some of the newer servants took Aunt Maddie's side. "Let's go, then" I said.

In the carriage, I sat unable to take it all in. Uncle 'Vester had, at one stroke, freed me from the power of Aunt Maddie. In a professor's house there would be marvelous books to read and I'd have money of my own. I wouldn't have to cheat Aunt Maddie out of enough money to do the things I wanted to do. I regarded it as wages for all the work I did around the house, but if Aunt Maddie ever knew of my sources of income she'd be outraged.

The basket of food which I had put in the carriage had not only the official calf's foot jelly which Aunt Maddie sent, but enough food from our kitchen to keep the Armitages eating for a week or two. Aunt Maddie would be scandalized at how much of what she had paid for was in that basket, and the little 'complements' the food merchants sent for our patronage went straight into my pockets since they knew that I made up the shopping lists and chose which merchants to patronize.

When we arrived at the shabby street where the Armitages lived, Thomas told me "You just send one of the boys for me when you're ready to go, Miss Vicky. No need to come to me." I simply said "I'll see" and slipped out of the coach. My freedom from supervision on these trips was very valuable to me: if I wanted to wander a bit after my visit to the Armitages it was easier to go to the public house and send in one of the horse-holders to get Thomas.

Robin was waiting at the door, and after I entered she gave me a hug. "It's so nice to see you, Vicky" she said. "My mother's lying down; she won't disturb us." I sighed. "Drunk again?" I said. "Where does she get the money?" Robin shook her head. "They keep a slate for her at the pub" she said. "I have to hide half the things you bring to keep her from paying the pub with your food. She probably got credit on the strength of the calf's-foot jelly you've brought: the publican's wife has a taste for it. What's new: you look so happy."

I sighed: this was going to be one of the disadvantages of my wonderful news. "I'm to leave Aunt Maddie's and go to Oxford to live with another aunt" I said. "Oh, Vicky," Robin cried, "how wonderful for you...but I'll miss you." There were tears in her eyes but she was trying to be brave. I hugged her. "Oxford is not all that far from London. If I can't get back to you, perhaps you can come up and visit me. I don't think Aunt Margot is going to be anything like Aunt Maddie; she'll probably allow me to have visitors."

Robin shook her head. "With you gone, I'll have to get work of some kind. I don't think I'll have much time for visiting." Suddenly an idea I'd sometimes thought of came almost fully developed into my mind. "I've got a job for you, Robin, and it won't use up as much of your time as an ordinary job. I think I can persuade Aunt Maddie to let you to take on a lot of the things I do at our house. She'll only do it if you don't take any wages, but I'll let you in on all my ploys: you can collect the 'complements' from the tradesmen and lots of other ways I have of making money. You won't have to live in: your excuse will be that you have to take care of your mother. And if you need to get away for a few days you can send a message that she's sick and needs you

Robin said slowly, "I always said I'd die before going into service, but I don't know how else I'd earn enough money to take care of Mother. Of course, this wouldn't really be going into service..." I shook my head. "Of course it isn't. You'll be an impoverished young lady helping out with some of the family affairs, supposedly out of gratitude for all those jars of calf's-foot jelly and the Bible reading. Besides, it would be such a waste if no one took over my money making schemes. But you will have to put up with Aunt Maddie."

She giggled. "The hardest part of that will be remembering not to call her Aunt Maddie to her face. I'm a much more successful hypocrite than you, Vicky. You can pretend to be submissive, but somehow you aren't really convincing. Your real feelings somehow come out in your attitude. I've *learned* to be a successful hypocrite, not only because of keeping Mother's drinking a secret, but also because it's the only way to get charity from people like your aunt. Until you started helping us, we were really in a bad state. As for your aunt, I'll 'flatter her to the top of her bent'."

"Well, don't let her know how well you know Shakespeare then" I said. Suddenly her whole demeanor changed; she seemed meek and submissive as Aunt Maddie wished *me* to be. "Oh, I couldn't read Mr. Shakespeare" she said in a voice I almost didn't recognize. "My Mother says that some parts of his works are *quite* improper." She even looked paler than usual, I thought, and she seemed more insignificant in appearance than she usually did. Then she laughed and her usual appearance came back, an air of jaunty independence. "And, of course, Mother *loves* the improper parts of Shakespeare."

"It's such a pity, Robin," I said, "your Mother is such a delightful person when she isn't drinking..." Robin shook her head. "No, nowadays, if she isn't drinking, she's miserable. When she first begins to drink she's, as you say, delightful. But if she keeps drinking...well, she's not so delightful; then, eventually, she'll fall asleep for a good many hours, sometimes sleeping the clock around. She's gotten worse since you first met us. If by taking on some of your duties I can make it easy for you to get away, I'll be happy to do it. With even a few shillings I can pay someone to keep an eye on her when I'm away."

"I think it will work out" I said. "Let's go walk in the park and I'll instruct you in all the ways I have of making money." We set off for the park: both of us knew how to dress and act so that we would be taken for a couple of working class girls on a brief holiday from jobs or other responsibilities. Robin's Cockney accent was better than mine, but I had a quicker wit in discouraging unwanted advances. My completely fictional brother, who was a bare-knuckle boxer had sent off a lot of overly persistent men: they weren't entirely sure of his existence, but it was no use taking chances.

When I got back to the house it was supper time and Aunt Maddie did not care to upset her digestion by flying into a temper at supper or immediately after. When I was summoned to her presence the next morning, her first fit of anger had died down and she was willing to listen to my suggestion about poor little Roberta Armitage, whom I had been teaching about my duties after our Bible reading. "Roberta would so much like to repay all your kindness to herself and her mother by taking over my duties here, Aunt Stone," I said. "She is so much alone with her ailing mother that she would really enjoy the company of gentlefolk while doing what I do. I'm sure Aunt Celia will soon grow fond of her."

Aunt Maddie hesitated but eventually gave her consent to the scheme. Not only would she have another person to dominate, but it would cost her nothing, except a few meals. "She may have her noon meal with the Family," she said. "After all, her mother is a distant connection of ours. And if her mother can be left with a neighbor to keep an eye on her, Miss Armitage will profit by keeping busy: idle hands are the devil's workshop." When I brought Robin in for an interview her meek, almost groveling, demeanor at once gained Aunt Maddie's approval.

Aunt Ceal was less easy to convince. "But what will I do without you," she said; "my books..." I told her soothingly, "Roberta has a very nice reading voice, and

The Gryphon Seal

if you give her the usual amount of money, she can get the books from the lending library for you." I charged Aunt Ceal about four times what the lending library charged me, especially since she insisted that I read her the latest 'woman's novels' from the library and could only be cajoled into letting me read her anything good, like Jane Austen, only once in a great while. As soon as she learned that her little conspiracy with me to obtain and read to her books which Aunt Maddie would completely disapprove of, she cheered up. I sometimes wondered how deep her emotions went: would she, indeed, miss *me* or only the indulgences which I helped her get? In her own way, Aunt Ceal was just as selfish as her sister. I was very glad that my dear Mama had been different, an opinion which was borne out, not only by my own memories, but also by the affection that the older servants in the house had for her. I also remembered warmly how Uncle 'Vester had said she was his favorite among his brother's children.

In the event, my uncle not only sent a carriage, but came himself to escort me. We had a good conversation on the journey to Oxford: he shared some memories of my mother and I asked him about some of his military exploits.

He looked at me with renewed respect. "Most of my junior officers don't know half as much about the history of my campaigns as you do, my dear," he said. "Your Aunt Maddie wouldn't approve of your interests, you know." He laughed, "Do you know that your mother gave those two their nicknames? She called Aunt Maddie that because she was always angry and Aunt Ceal because she was always silly enough to be dominated by Aunt Maddie. Do you know what your Aunt Stone's proper name is?"

"My Mama told me it's Magdalene." I said. "She's so offended by the name that she never uses it: even on legal documents she signs herself Miss M. Stone, and relatives are required to call her Aunt or Cousin Stone." He laughed a little grimly. "Well, you're free of her and her attitudes now and I think we can keep you free. Here's a Banker's Order on Barclay's Bank for this quarter; you'll know how to deal with it. I think you're quite capable of helping your Aunt Margot without hurting her pride. She's a darling, but she has plenty of the family pride".

Chapter Two

Aunt Margot was indeed a darling, but very frail; so frail that I decided that my first job would be to build her up. Her finances were somewhat frail, too, but after a quick look at the Banker's Order which Uncle 'Vester had given me, I knew I could help there. Uncle 'Vester's ideas about what constituted a quarter's allowance for a relative must have been based on what he had received from *his* father, or given to his sons; it was totally disproportionate for what most women with estates received. I wondered if I really had the funds in my father's estate to justify this much of an allowance or whether Uncle 'Vester had quietly added to the amount, for Margot's sake as well as mine.

One of the first things Aunt Margot had told me was just to call her Margot (Which she pronounced in the French way with the silent "t" not the more English Margott). "Being called 'Aunt' makes me feel so old, my dear" she said. "I know I am old, but I don't want to feel old. I'm sorry to bring you into this disorganized household. Neither Petty not I had much common sense, but Petty had all that there was in our family. Dear Sylvester says you'll be able to help: says you're quite practical and intelligent. He says 'you've got your head screwed on well' -- such a funny expression. Are you interested in words and phrases, dear? Petty and I both were -- it was one of the many things we had in common."

"I'm very interested in words and phrases," I said, "and I envy Uncle Pettigrew's knowledge of Greek: I'd love to learn Greek." Margot smiled at me. "Oh,

I can teach you Greek, all right" she said surprisingly. "Petty often had me tutor his students who hadn't properly learned Greek at public school but showed promise in other ways. I'll teach you Greek and you can take over the management of the household. Does that sound like a good bargain to you? It does to me, but then I value Greek more than most people".

It sounded like an excellent bargain to me, especially since I ached to be able to run a household with no interference. We needed a cook and someone to help with the rough cleaning, I thought. By walking up and down the road Margot's house was on and looking for the best kept house, I found my way to the back door of one that had impressed me. "I'm sorry to disturb you," I told the matronly figure who answered the door. I'm Victoria Marsdon and I'm staying with my Aunt Margot down the road..."

"The Professor's widow?" the woman cried out. "I'm so glad she has someone staying with her. She and the Professor were the salt of the earth. Well, she still is you know, but they went so well together. But you should be at the front door, miss, though my mistress is taking her nap."

"It's really you I wanted to see" I said. "My aunt and I will need a cook who doesn't insist on a scullery maid and someone to do the rough cleaning". She smiled. "Ah, well, that's my department, Miss Victoria. I'm Mrs. Fuller, Lady Tansham's cook. I think I may be able to help you out -- my sister's retired now and sometimes the rheumatics bother her, but she doesn't like being idle. Cooking for two ladies, even without a scullery maid is just what she'd like; and Mrs. Stockton, who does our rough cleaning, should be able to fit you in; I know she has time free. Come in, my dear, and have a cup of tea, if you're not too proud. And come around the front door next time. I know my lady will be very glad to meet you. She was a redhead in her youth, and she's always partial to redheaded women."

"I'm certainly not too proud to come into a kitchen that smells like this," I said, "and I'd love a cup of tea." One of the first things I had done in Margot's house was to wash out the pomade from my hair and my locks were now very red and very uncontrolled. Margot loved it and I was gradually getting used to it.

Mrs. Fuller was a kindly soul and the state of cleanliness and order in the kitchen more than bore out my first impression that this was a well run house. She pressed fresh baked scones on me, and when I left insisted that I take a covered plate of them to Margot. "Tell her that Mrs. Fuller is sorry for her troubles" she said. "She's a lovely lady, and I think her luck has turned with you coming to stay with her. I'll send my sister to you tomorrow, and Mrs. Stockton on Wednesday when she comes, unless you'd like her sooner."

"You're a gem and a jewel, Mrs. Fuller" I said. "I'm so glad that I came to you." She looked at me curiously. "If you'll excuse me, Miss, why did you?" she said. I laughed. "The windows were so clean and the curtains looked so fresh, and I could see the herb garden at the side of the yard." I said. She shook her head. "I can see you're related to the professor," she said. "Head in the clouds most of the time, but every so often he'd come out with such a shrewd, practical idea that you could see he had a head on him. It was nice to meet you, Miss Victoria. You come to the front door next time and the girl who lets you in will be Edie, who keeps the windows so clean. She'll recognize you, all right; not many red tops like yours."

I went back to Margot's house, which I was already beginning to think of as our house, and gave Margot scones and tea for our teatime. "And you've already arranged about servants" she said admiringly". I can see that Sylvester was right about you. But you'll need more food later on, a healthy young girl like you. When Petty died, I let the cook and her sister go to a better job..." I said "Don't worry, Margot. There's plenty of food left in the kitchen: a whole big ham and some good cheese. Would you like me to fix you anything?" She shook her head. "I'm stuffed with these delicious scones" she said. "And I'm going to bed to catch up on my sleep, now you're here to take care of things."

In the following week or so, things shook down very well. Mrs. MacDonald, our cook, had much more of a Scot's Brogue than her sister, Mrs. Fuller, who had lived in England most of her life. Mrs. Stockton was a displaced Cockney, who loved talking about London with me. When I understood her Cockney idioms and even some of her rhyming slang , I won her heart easily. I discharged several tradesmen who wanted overly high prices for things like eggs and milk and bread, and hired people who Mrs. Fuller recommended. My Greek lessons went swimmingly: Margot was a fine teacher, and she had books that she had used to tutor her husband's students.

Besides organizing the household, I read to Margot: we started with Jane Austen's *Emma* by mutual agreement. "There's nothing seriously wrong with my eyes, Vicky," she told me, "but a year ago I had what physicians call a stroke, and it seemed to rob me of the ability to read. Petty was so good about it: he'd read to me every night. I think I'm getting back to being able to read again, and familiar things, like the Greek texts I used to instruct Petty's students, are easier than unfamiliar things. After we finish *Emma* you choose the next book; I'm sure you'll find something interesting". After years of reading silly romances to Aunt Ceal, it was a delightful situation.

I got fairly frequent reports from Robin by half-penny post about the situation at Aunt Maddie's house. So far, Robin hadn't put a foot wrong and Aunt Maddie was comparing Robin favorably to me. "Perhaps you are a better person than I" I wrote Robin and she replied, "Nonsense, Vicky, you just have too much integrity to flatter and cozen your aunt as I do. She's not *my* aunt and I don't care what I say to her, so long as I get what I want. She's even condescendingly kind about my Mother, but much too proud and lazy to come to our house, as you told me she would be. Solange isn't so bad, if you'll gossip with her about the neighbors. Mrs. Varley is the only citadel still unwon."

With things settling down to this highly pleasant routine, I began to look around me a little. Margot was getting stronger, but still spent a lot of time resting. I could leave the running of the household to Mrs. MacDonald and Mrs. Stockridge. A few days after I arrived, I had walked to Barclay's bank, asked to see the manager and gave him my Banking Order. Mr. Treddinge was a tall, slender man whose age was hard to guess,. but he had considerable shrewdness behind his eyes. "Your great-uncle General Athlone evidently trusts you a great deal, putting this amount at your disposal, Miss Marsden" he said. "He's a shrewd man and I'll trust you, too. I'll put this amount in an account which will earn you interest, and give you some cheques which will be honored by our bank. However, there is a problem about cheques signed with a woman's name, though Lady Tansham gets away with it..."

"I'll make the signature 'V. Marsden'" I said, signing the sheet he gave me. "You might write a note which I can carry saying that I am authorized to sign such checques if I have to do it personaly." He nodded. "I think two letters, Miss Marsden; one saying that you may pay bills with these checques and the other saying that you are authorized to sign them. The second letter should be produced only when it is necessary. A fine signature, Miss Marsden. Not many people would think it was a woman's signature, if you'll forgive me for saying so."

"It is rather flamboyant" I said, deciding not to be offended. "My father helped me to develop it. He said a signature tells a great deal about you." He looked at me appraisingly. "As a banker, I would have to agree" he said. "You're Victor Marsden's daughter, I believe. Would you like to see his signature?" "Why, yes," I said, startled. He took out a package of what looked like a subscription list from a box on the table and said, "Perhaps you'd be interested in this." He held out a list of five hundred pound contributions, signed with my father's equally flamboyant signature. It was made out to a man named Arthur Evans.

The Gryphon Seal

"How do you happen to have this?" I asked. "We have Mr. Evans' personal account here" he said. "I've been working on it since the late Professor Pettigrew left Mr. Evans some money. Both he and your father were supporting Mr. Evans' excavations on Crete. Mr. Evans is the curator - they call him the Keeper - of the Ashmolean Museum. He has been excavating in Crete for some years now, at a site named Knossos." Something in the words "Evans" and "Knossos" seemed somehow very important to me.

"I'll have to ask Aunt Margot about Mr. Evans" I said. "Anyone whom both my father and Uncle Pettigrew supported must be an interesting man." He nodded slowly. "Your mother was Elizabeth Stone" he said. I stared at him. "Why, yes," I said, "but how did you know that?" He hesitated. "I knew your mother many years ago" he said. "Like all who knew her well, I valued her highly. Her death and your father's were indeed a tragedy." I rose. "Yes" I said. "Is that all I need to do here now?" There was just too much unexpected stress in this meeting: I'd better leave before I started crying or disgraced myself in some other way. "I'll send the checques to Mrs. Pettigrew's house by a bank messenger. And Miss Victoria, if I can be of any help to you in any matter, please call on me." I murmured "Thank you" and made rapidly for the door.

When I got home, I shared this strange experience with Margot. She looked surprised, but not amazed. "John Treddings, yes: his family has been in banking for a long time. I didn't know he was manager of the Oxford branch of Barclays. He was one of the men who were very attracted to your mother. But then Victor came along and she had no eyes for anyone but him."

I shied away from this talk about my parents: I hadn't really realized how thinking of their deaths still hurt. "Do you know this Arthur Evans?" I asked. She laughed. "Oh, Goggles Evans, dear, of course I do. He wears enormous spectacles and he can hardly see even with them. But he's been all over the world, exploring, helping fighters for freedom, writing about the things he's seen. Then around the end of the Queen's reign, he bought the place at Knossos, near Candia, in Crete, got himself appointed Keeper at the Ashmolean, and has spent almost every summer in Crete, excavating a marvelous site, revealing a totally forgotten part of history. Come into Petty's study; I'm sure we have some things of his."

After a brief search she came up with a box addressed to my Uncle Pettigrew. "I know we have some of his books and reports, but I'm too tired to look for them now. These are some artifacts that he sent to Petty, not long before he died. Petty, of course, not Goggles. I'm not sure that Petty ever looked at it--he was failing even then. But look at the things in it: it may give you some idea of the things he's excavating. I suppose when he gets back in a few weeks we should give the things back to him. Oh, dear, it brings Petty and his enthusiasms back so vividly. Good night, Vicky."

I didn't want to think about my parents any more than she wanted to think about her lost husband, so I turned to the little box in an effort to distract my mind. It was a solidly constructed wooden box with interior compartments stuffed with interesting objects. There were some oddly, but beautifully, shaped cups, a clay model of a bull, some fragments of pottery with beautiful designs on them, and in a small compartment, what looked like a ring. I lifted out the ring, which was the least breakable object that I could see.

It was of gold, with a design of some kind incised on it. It looked like a seal ring which my father had with the Marsden family crest on it: by pressing it into sealing wax, you could impress the design onto the wax. But the design on this one was not a family crest, but a strange kind of animal. At first I thought it was ugly, but looking more closely at it, I discovered a strange new kind of beauty. It was an animal with a lion's body, wings on its back, and the head of an eagle, except the head had what looked like ears, and riding on the back of the animal was a human figure. A gryphon! That's what it was: I had seen gryphons, or griffins, as some spelled it, on English coats of arms.

The figure on the back could have been a boy, but as I looked more closely, I saw that it was definitely a girl, and clad only in a short tunic, her legs and upper body unclothed. There were definitely breasts I could see, looking at it closely. My aunts would have called it indecent, but there was nothing indecent about it. The girl looked proud and free and there was nothing sexual about the figure except the proudly flaunted breasts. Moved by some impulse that seemed to come from deep within me, I slipped the ring onto my finger.

Suddenly, the light of the room seemed to fail; it grew darker and darker. I stood up and began to grope my way to the door, but in the darkness it seemed that I had come much farther than the door of the room could be, much farther than the whole space within the room, or even the house. I groped my way forward, and at last there was some light ahead of me. I went towards the light and was suddenly blinded by a light like the noonday sun. But it *was* the noonday sun, even though Margot had shown me the box after supper and I had looked at the chest by lamplight.

Suddenly I tripped over something and fell bruisingly to the floor. But it wasn't a floor, carpeted as most downstairs rooms in Margot's house were, but bare wooden planks. I looked around as my eyes adjusted to the sunlight and saw that I was on the deck of a ship, a strange old fashioned ship with a single sail and oarlocks at the sides of the ship. The sun was bright, almost tropical, and what looked like the crew were wearing topless tunics like the girl on the ring. All around me was the surging sea, nothing solid but this little sailing ship, and all around, a sparkling ocean, with no land in sight, a tropical, or at least Mediterranean ocean, an ocean which did not exist within hundreds of miles of Oxford!

Chapter Three

The crew members, as I thought they must be, turned away to their ropes and sail, seeing that I had only taken a tumble as any landlubber aboard a small ship. I burned with indignation: I was a *good* sailor! My father had told me so when he had taken me sailing when I was a child in his yacht not a great deal smaller than this boat. A tall, lanky man in a grayish wool tunic, which covered his upper body and not just his lower body, loomed over me. "Are you all right?" he asked. "You've been seasick for so long it's best to move cautiously at first."

"I was not seasick!" I insisted and he grinned, "Well, it certainly looked like seasickness to me, but perhaps it was only the shock of being plucked away from your home and sent on this ship to Crete. Do you remember anything about that?" I spoke slowly. "I don't really think I do." He sat down cross-legged beside me on the deck. "You're memory will come back: it's been quite a shock for us all. I'm Artimadorus. What's your name?" I said slowly, "It's Vicky -- or at least that's what my friends call me." A memory brushed my mind; a kindly older man who had said "my friends call me..." What?... "Vester" I thought, "Uncle 'Vester". Artimadorus looked at me a little anxiously. "Don't try to remember: I'll just tell you how we got here. They brought out all of the youths and maidens of Athens and the strange priestess with the snake, chose some of us to come to Crete. This is a Cretan ship, as you can tell by the crew's clothing and the octopus design on the sail."

Suddenly a thought struck me and I glanced down at my body. I was respectably clad in a long robe something like a night-shift, thank heavens. I remembered wistfully the proud young body on the ring, but something made me turn the bezel of the ring inward so only the thin gold of the ring itself showed.

"They hustled us to the ship and some few parents managed to get a few possessions to their children. There are seven boys and seven girls, you know. A lot of them are still seasick or in a shocked state. Even though you took a tumble, you're on your feet more quickly than most. Did your parents get anything to you?" he asked. "My parents are dead" I said flatly. "I'm sorry" he said, and he did sound sorry.

"There are all kinds of wild rumors about what's going to happen to us when we reach Crete, but I believe we're going to be part of some religious ceremony, or game, or perhaps both, which involves what they call 'the Dance'. And there's a bull involved in it somehow." "A religious ceremony, or a game, or perhaps both." My aunt would sneer at that: she was against all sorts of gaming and the religious ceremonies she took part in had nothing to do with games or dancing. My aunt's name was...what? I wasn't just pretending not to remember; I realized that I *really* couldn't remember.

"You look skeptical" said Artimadorus, "you have a very expressive face." I said slowly "I live with an aunt. She...wouldn't understand how something could be a dance and a game and a religious ceremony all at the same time." He nodded. "My mother was a priestess of the virgin hunter before her family had her released to marry and have a son. Some people think

The Gryphon Seal

that's a rather gloomy worship: the priestesses have to be virgins and some of the rituals are rather ferocious. You seem surprised."

"My aunt wouldn't like people talking about virgins" I said. A voice came from behind me "She's a prude; that's not a religion, that's a disability." I looked up and saw a tall dark haired girl who had come up behind us. I rose to my feet. "This is Vicky" said Artimadorus. She's the next on her feet." The dark girl smiled in a friendly way. "I'm Helena" she said. "I'm not as bad as I sound--sometimes. I don't remember you at home." I said "I live with my aunt--she doesn't like me going out too much." Helena nodded. "I feel sorry for people like that. Won't have any fun themselves and are dead set against other people having fun.

"Look, Artimadorus," she said. " I've had an idea about why we were chosen. You have a cousin who was taken in the first contingent, don't you?" Artimadorus nodded. "Yes, Menesthius" he said. "He's the son of a priest and a good fellow." Helena said in a low tone "A lot of the girls here used to be friends with Alceme, who was taken in the first contingent. You say Menesthius is a good fellow, and I'd trust Alceme pretty far. I wonder if our being chosen by that priestess with the snake wasn't something planned by those two. You're a beast-wizard, aren't you? You can do what you like with animals." Artimadorus nodded. "Most of the time" he said, "but I tried to take control of that snake and the priestess took it back. She's a better beast-wizard than I am."

Helena nodded. "Well, beast-wizards are not all that uncommon, though you're better than most, and that girl is better than you. Anyway, if we were chosen because Menesthius knows you and Alceme knows me and many of the other girls as well, it looks like someone has a plan involving us and I don't think Menesthius or Alceme would bring us into a situation that was bad for us. Maybe dangerous -- Alceme was a real daredevil -- but not in the long run a *bad* situation."

Artimadorus nodded. "I think there's something in what you say, but there's some kind of emergency affecting this crew. That priestess isn't on board and another important man stayed behind, too. And we're sailing as fast as we possibly can: sailing until it gets too dark to see. Something's up."

"Well, we'd better be prepared for it then." said Helena. "Come on, Vicky, help me rouse the other girls and Artimadorus, go light a fire under the boys." She led me away, chatting amiably; somehow she reminded me of a friend I once had. The name 'Robin' came to me, but somehow it sounded a little strange. We did rouse the girls and Artimadorus the boys, and it was just as well because before too long we hove to and the seven youths and seven maidens were transferred to smaller boats while the ship went off at a right angle to our previous course. Helena and I were in the same boat and I earned her respect by not being seasick and telling her some things to do to avoid it. Facing up to the wind and breathing deeply helped a lot, while those who huddled in the bottom of the boat were soon sicker than they had been on the ship.

Eventually we got to port and Helena stared at a figure waiting for us on the dock. "That's my friend, Alceme," she said, "But look at how she's dressed."

The Gryphon Seal

The girl she was pointing to was dressed very much like the figure on my seal stone, in a short tunic which left her top bare, and very little else. Not only did she seem completely comfortable in this clothing, but the people around her seemed highly respectful of her. When she snapped out an order in a string of strange words people jumped to obey her, bringing our boat to the dock at her feet.

"Hello Helena" she said cheerfully. "Look at what they're wearing this year. Who's your friend?" Helena gulped. "This is Vicky; she's a good sailor" she said, which pleased me. "What are these clothes for? A party -- or an orgy?" Alceme shook her head. "These are Dancer's kilts: they're working clothes, my dear, and people respect us for wearing them. I'm going to teach you ,and perhaps your friend too, to leap over bulls. It's hard work, but very gratifying." Helena took a deep breath. "Leaping over bulls -- sounds like you. Are we going to leap them together?"

Alceme shook her head. "No, you're my replacement: I'll tell you why later. I'm sorry you had a rough voyage. One of our neighboring islands is threatened by a fire mountain and every one of our ships is hastening to take the people off before the mountain blows. You can see the plume of the fire mountain over there." She lifted her hand and pointed: you could see a trail of smoke going up to the sky. We could probably seen it from the ship or the boat, but we were only concerned with where we were going, not anything along the way.

" Our ships" I said on an impulse. Alceme smiled at me. "Clever girl, to catch that. Yes, this is my home now. I've chosen the man I'll marry here and this will be my home for as long as he stays here. You two might make the same choice: it's a much better place for a woman than Athens." Helena said "If I get to dress like that and people admire me for it instead of shaming me, I'm pretty sure I'll like it here." Alceme shook her head. "It's what you do in these clothes that people admire you for, not the clothes themselves. Not that most men don't gaze at you, but it takes a bold man to make a move on a bull-girl, much less a Leaper like me. Some of your friends still look pretty seasick: they'll be carried on litters to the House. Why don't you and Vicky walk up with me; it will loosen up your muscles." Somewhere in he back of my mind I thought that my aunt would be outraged at the idea of a woman *having* muscles, much less 'loosening them up.

Alceme looked at me with curiosity. "The - ah - priestess chose you with the snake?" she asked, "So I'm told" I said. She said, half aloud, "You weren't on my list - I wonder..." Helena jumped on this. "You did have a list, then" she said. "I thought you were behind it when so many of our old gang were chosen by the priestess. Some of them are married already, or live outside Athens." Alceme nodded. "So Chryseis had to choose substitutes then." she said. "Well, your friend, Vicky, seems a good choice. She passed the first test, not getting seasick. Sailors are always impressed by that. They say it shows that you have the blood of one of the gods in you. By the time I got over mine Chr... a friend of mine had all the men on the ship paying attention to her. It wasn't until I became a Leaper that I began to get what I regarded as my proper share of admiration, and by that time N'suto and I were getting serious and it didn't matter any more."

I cast a sidelong glance at her. She had blonde hair, which contrasted with the darker hair of most of the Cretans who shared the path with us, and in the brief 'kilt' she made a spectacular figure. I found it hard to believe that she hadn't always had her share of male attention. My aunt would have called her a "shameless hussy", but to me she didn't give that impression.

When we reached what Alceme called the House, it turned out to be an immense hive of buildings surrounded by a village of smaller houses. Alceme led us along one edge of the palace and said to us "Let's see if Ariadne is on the practice court." She led us through a sort of hedge to a long court, surrounded by further hedges. Another girl in a kilt was there. She had black hair, so dark that it looked almost blue in some lights; she and Alceme made a spectacular pair. "Oh, there you are, Alceme" she said. "Are these some of your friends who've come from Athens in the new draft?" Alceme smiled. "One old friend and one new one" she said. "Can you run the bull for me, Ariadne, so I can show them what's involved in the Dance?" The dark haired girl smiled. "Just as I did with Chryseis when she first came? Well, why not." She lifted her hand and gave a piercing whistle. From some hedges at one end of the court, two men led out a bull, guiding it with cords wrapped around its horns. The dark haired girl gave another signal and the men whipped the cords from the bull's horns and it began to run toward us. I saw Helena move uneasily beside me, but I stood rooted to the spot, looking at the magnificent spectacle of the running bull. Alceme ran toward the bull, grabbed its horns and when the bull tossed its head she sailed over its head, landed on its back and somersaulted off. "Oh, well," said Ariadne. She ran toward the bull and did a similar leap with what seemed like even greater skill. Ariadne ran to one side of the court and Alceme to the opposite side. The bull skidded to a stop, turned around and raced down the court again. As it passed the two girls, both of them leaped for the broad back and did a handstand on it for a moment, before somersaulting off the opposite side. For one thrilling moment, their bodies were perfectly aligned as they did their simultaneous handstands on the bull's back.

The bull ran back to the two men who had led it out, who captured it and led it away. "I thought that you couldn't resist jumping, too." said Alceme to Ariadne. "Believe it or not, ladies, but this sort of thing becomes an addiction: it's hard to stop once you've become skilled at it. Ariadne is one of the best leapers in the world and I'm not too bad at it." Ariadne shook her head and said "You're quite good enough not to fish for compliments, Alceme, but Chryseis is better than either of us."

"Well, I've followed you into some strange places" said Helena to Alceme. "I suppose I can follow you over a bull's back." I said slowly "I don't know if I can do it, but, oh, how I'd like to."

"Wanting to is half the battle" said Ariadne to me with a smile. "I'm quite sure that you and your friend can learn to Leap. But of course the Leaping is only part of the Dance: there's a whole ritual that both the Leapers and the ground dancers have to learn. It's hard work, but as Alceme says, it has its rewards. You won't go into training for a while though. Did Alceme tell you about the fire mountain on Dariapane? Most of the Dancers are running errands connected with receiving refugees; a Dancer in her kilt makes a pretty spectacular appearance, and people are used to respecting them and obeying them. I suppose that Chryseis stayed with the ship when it dropped you off? Did the priestess who picked you out stay on board?" she asked Helena and me.

Helena shook her head. "She and one of the men got left behind for some reason" she said. "At least that was what some of the people on the ship were saying." In response to a rather stricken look from Ariadne, Alceme said bracingly "It's no use worrying, Ariadne. I'm almost as fond of Chryseis as you are, but as I concluded long ago, she's a tough as old leather under all that girlish charm. That one can fall into a barrel of stinking fish and come up with a flower in her teeth. I rather suspect that she's made her way to Aegina: they're good sailors there and they have a lot of respect for her mother. I'll bet you she'll be here before too long on an Aeginian ship with a load of refugees.

"Well, perhaps," said Ariadne, and I realized that under their friendly attitude was a sharp edge of rivalry involving the mysterious Chryseis. I didn't know quite where I was or what I was doing there, but I realized that under their strange clothing and strange skills these two women were not all that different from women I had known in my earlier life. That somehow made me feel a little more at home. The poet was right: "One touch of nature makes the whole world kin."

Alceme was right: Chryseis did eventually come back on an Aegean ship loaded with refugees, but after a great many adventures which were not shared with Helena or me until much later. Presently the stream of refugees dwindled to a mere trickle and we began our training. The training for the Dancers had three separate divisions. All of us had to learn the dance proper, where we filed onto the great central court in the palace, singing and making ritual movements to the music of flutes and drums, and when the Leaping was done, we left the court in a similar way. Those of us who were or might become Leapers had additional training, practicing leaps, first over training dummies and then over actual bulls. The tauromath, the beast wizard who actually controlled the bull, had to undergo additional training with Ariadne or Chryseis controlling the bull with their minds so that it did the required movements, tossing its head in a straight line rather than to one side or the other and running up the court and returning again.

All these were hard for us, though of course, only Artimadorus took the last kind of training. I was totally unused to making the ritual movements and singing in unison with them: nothing in my life with Aunt Maddie had prepared me for this kind of performance. The Athenian youths had evidently done something similar in ceremonies honoring Athena, the patroness of their city, but for me, religion meant going to a gloomy church, trying to sing hymns from a hymn book and listening to a long, almost always boring sermon.

The Gryphon Seal

Gradually I found myself learning the movements of the Dance, and I noticed with others, and even in myself, we were beginning to move, even outside the Dance, with a certain grace and style. Some Cretans mentioned something about a 'dancer's grace' and I could see that I and my companions were beginning to acquire this.

The training for Leaping was hard in a different way. When under Aunt Maddie's eye, I had to 'act like a lady' which definitely did not include any physical activity such as jumping and running. I could remember wild romps with my parents before they had gone on their yachting trip and never returned, but I was confined at my aunt's house to small 'ladylike' movements, showing no strength or skill.

Such movements were forced on women of my class by being bound up in corsets with whalebone stays. It made it very hard to do any physical activity at all and led to young women 'swooning'; losing consciousness because of the construction of the corset. I had always fiercely resisted even putting on one of these horrible things and since I am fairly slimly built and had no chance to get any fat on my bones on what Aunt Maddie fed us, I got away with it. As Dancers, we were proud of our slender waists, and the men especially tightened their belts to show how slender they were. That was part of the image we had as dancers: It went along with smooth muscles and a complete mastery of movement. By the time I had learned a little of the Cretan language and found my way to other parts of the palace after our training sessions, I was so used to wearing the kilt that I felt no self consciousness.

When we began to leap actual bulls instead of dummies, I had another problem. My parents had liked animals, but because they spent a lot of their time traveling we didn't have a family dog or even a family cat. When I went to live with Aunt Maddie, there was never an animal allowed in the house: not even a kitchen cat. And at one time I had been frightened by a barking dog who nipped at me and might have bitten me if Tom Coachman hadn't chased him away: luckily I was just getting into the carriage.

As a result, I had no experience of animals and was rather afraid of the bigger ones. A Leaping bull is very definitely a formidable beast, even when firmly controlled by a tauromath, so Helena overcame her fears quicker that I did and took Alceme's place in actual Dances before I was ready. There was some hurry: Alceme was pregnant by her Cretan lover, whom she would marry when he came back from a sea trading voyage. I actually had to replace Chryseis in the Dance which made me even more nervous. But the day came when I was already and Chryseis disappeared on some mysterious errand of her own.

Artimadorus had a different kind of problem becoming the tauromath of our troupe. Both Ariadne and Chryseis had complete control of the bull, helped apparently by some religious or magical ceremony which they had undergone. For some reason, Artimadorus couldn't undergo this ceremony and he had to keep stretching and training his natural power over animals to take Chryseis' place as tauromath. Thank heavens, I was only required to replace her as one of the two female Leapers, not as Tauromath.

I never got anywhere close to the skill of Alceme or Ariadne, much less that of Chryseis, and I never did do the 'head leap', the leap over the bull's horns, but I did become a Leaper and did quite a creditable 'side leap', the one where you leap over the bull from the side as Alceme and Ariadne had that first day. I never did quite understand the political situation either, except that Minos, the ruler of Crete, hated Athenians and was trying to get back at them by using the Dance.

Antemadorus eventually became the 'tauromath' of our group; the beast-wizard who controls the bull. He was also my first male friend. Then one day in practice, I missed my footing, crashed into the bull's side and fell heavily. As I lost consciousness, I remember thinking what a stupid mistake it had been.

Chapter Four

When I woke up, I saw Margot at the end of my bed, looking into my face anxiously. "Oh, you finally woke up Vicky. We've all been so worried about you. Do you remember what happened? The gas jet in the study went out and you seem to have fallen in trying to make your way to the door. That wouldn't have been so bad, but the gas came back on and started filling the study. If Mrs. MacDonald hadn't smelled it and gotten up to see where the gas was coming from and found you, you might have been asphyxiated! I'm so sorry Vicky. The whole gas system in the house really needs to be worked on, but Petty and I could never afford to do it."

"It's not your fault, Margot," I said, privately vowing to spend some of my allowance to have the gas system overhauled. "How long was I unconscious?" Margot said "Ever since last night, and it's early morning now. Are you sure you're all right? I was going to get dressed and go for Dr. Sampson, or send Mrs. Stockton when she got here." I smiled at them. "No, I'm perfectly all right; I don't even have a headache. But I would like a cup of tea." She hurried off and got it while I tried to readjust my whole outlook. When I had been in ancient Crete, I had difficulty in remembering my life in London and Oxford, but now I had no trouble in remembering what had happened to me in Crete.

And it had happened, I had no doubt of that. It was all too detailed and real to have been a vivid dream brought on by my fall and the gas which had accumulated in the room. Underneath my plans to have the gas system overhauled, I was wondering what the team would do without me and what had happened to Helena and my other friends. I wondered if I could still leap a bull, not that I'd ever get a chance in this time. Probably I could: I felt fitter than I ever had before my experience and my muscles seemed to have those moves somehow inside them. I wondered if my body had actually gone back to ancient Crete, or just some inner part of me. Speaking of bodies, mine seemed to be draped in a lot of unnecessary clothing: they hadn't undressed me except for my shoes, simply laid me on the bed in my own room.

I felt frowsty and rather dirty. I'd really like a bath, but it was not so easy a matter in this house: no servant girls to bring in the tub and pour warm water over your head. I'd have to light a device, called a geyser, in the big gloomy bathroom, and wait until it heated a small amount of water for the tub. Surely there must be more modern arrangements for bathing nowadays than could be found in this house or my Aunt's house. If I was going to have the gas system overhauled, maybe I could do something about that.

But a bath really would do me some good, and when Margot came back with my tea I told her so. She got some fresh towels while I struggled to light the geyser, which , as usual, produced a great deal of noise and very little hot water. I managed to get reasonably clean: I found that my experience in Crete had raised my standards of cleanliness. I padded back to my room in bare feet with the garments I had been wearing slung over my shoulder: only when I closed the door did it occur to me hew scandalized Mrs. Stockton would have been if she had seen me parading down the corridor "naked as a jaybird," as she would say, with my clothes draped over my shoulder.

When had I dressed in fresh clothing, I laid aside some of what seemed to me unnecessary undergarments: why on earth did women wear all of these petticoats and other inner garments? A court lady in Crete wore far more than a kilt, of course; elaborate flounced skirts and a sort of jacket that left their breasts exposed, but certainly not all these unnecessary corsets and bustiers. My experience in Crete had taken several months, enough time to make a lot of present day customs look rather strange.

When I came downstairs, I discovered one reason for the extra garments: it was chilly in the house. Margot saw me shivering and gave me a sort of surcoat she wore sometimes. It was wool and really helped with the rather chilly atmosphere. But the emotional atmosphere was far from chilly. "When you--well in my day they'd have called it a swoon--and I had to worry about you, Vicky, it really made me realize how much I owe you for coming here and taking over everything. Life is so much more comfortable for me now than it has been since Petty died. Is there anything I can do for you, child?"

"Well, there is one thing," I said. "There's a friend of mine in London that I'd like to have as a guest here for a few days." Margot said quickly, "Of course you can invite her. Write her today! Or even send a telegram!" I laughed. "Perhaps I will send a telegram. It would be a great event for her: she's probably never had a telegram--I know that I haven't." Mrs. Stockton was

The Gryphon Seal

sent off with money from Margot to send a telegram to Robin. I rather wished I could go instead: I'd not only never had a telegram, I'd never sent one. In fact, it struck me how little I'd been out of the house since I got to Oxford. When Robin came she and I could explore Oxford as we had London.

One thing I could do while waiting for the reply paid response was to visit the house where Mrs. Fuller was a cook--by the front door. I consulted Mrs. MacDonald about a good time to catch Lady Tansham "at home" and went to call.

The door was opened by a pretty young maid who said "I know who you are! Miss Victoria Marsden." I smiled at her. "Red hair is hard to disguise," I said. "Would you give the plate to Mrs. Fuller and announce me to Lady Tansham. And I do like the way you keep the windows so clean, Edie." She gave me a rather startled look and said "Fancy Mrs. Fuller telling you that, Miss. Well, my father cleans windows for a living and if I didn't do as well as I do, Dad would come down on me. Thank you Miss Victoria. I'll announce you to Lady Tansham." I smiled at her and said, "Thank you, Edie, and tell your father to call in at our house. Mrs. Stockton is a good soul, but she doesn't really do well at windows."

When I entered the drawing room, I thought for a moment that Lady Tansham was another like Aunt Maddie: she sat so erect and her gaze was so searching. Then she smiled, which Aunt Maddie would never do to a stranger, and said, "You not only have a red top, you flaunt it." I returned her smile. "I wasn't allowed to when I lived with my Aunt Stone in London, but

Margot doesn't mind at all." She looked at me keenly and said "You tell Margot Pettigrew that I'm heartily ashamed of not calling on her earlier, but I'm a coward. I knew how much Pettigrew meant to her and I didn't like intruding on her grief. Tell her I'll call next Thursday."

"I'm sure she'll be glad to see you, Lady Tansham, but I don't think you're a coward for not visiting her sooner. Many people would say that it was your finer feelings rather than cowardice which kept you from calling on Margot after her husband's death."

She snorted. "Fine feelings are too often an excuse for cowardice. You aren't all that impressed at meeting a 'Lady' are you?" she observed shrewdly. "Well, perhaps I'm not," I said honestly. "I'm impressed more by what people do than by their titles." My mind flew back to Ariadne, who was not only a fine Leaper and a good friend, but was the heiress to the throne of Crete: the man who married her would be the next ruler of Crete. I wasn't impressed by someone who had the title of "Lady" and didn't have much to show for it except pride and a condescending attitude to other people. "I'll tell you what did impress me. The banker Mr. Teddings at Barclay's bank said that you wrote your own checques and signed them with your own name."

"John Teddings had no business discussing that with you," Lady Tansham said. rather sharply. I felt obliged to defend Mr. Teddings, who had been kind. "It came up in connection with my account. General Athlone is making me an allowance and I've deposited it at Barclay's and can write checques on the amount."

The Gryphon Seal

She eyed me shrewdly. "The allowance must be fairly sizable or John wouldn't have dealt with it himself. You have interesting aspects, young Vicky. Would you like some tea, or perhaps a glass of sherry?" I hesitated and then said, "A glass of sherry, if you please, Lady Tansham. I've never had it before." I didn't mention that as a Leaper I'd not only been well fed but been given plenty of wine with my meals, well watered during the day when we were practicing and performing, but you could have it unmixed at night to help you sleep.

Lady Tansham rang the bell and told Edie to bring two glasses of the best sherry. I tried it cautiously and told Lady Tansham "I rather like it. It has a sort of nutty taste." Lots of the Cretan wines were rather sweet and tasted better well mixed with water, but I had developed a fondness for a kind of wine with a touch of pine-resin in it, which most of the Athenians disliked, but to me it had a nice, fresh taste, like drinking a pine tree.

"You continue to surprise me, child," Lady Tansham said. "Don't ask for sherry anywhere else you visit or you'll lose your reputation, but you can always have it here: I like sherry and don't like drinking alone. Let's drop the Lady Tansham business. My rather absurd name is Violet. If you call Mrs. Pettigrew 'Margot', you might as well call me 'Violet'--in private, of course."

`I laughed. "You're certainly no 'shrinking violet', but otherwise it suits you. A violet is really quite an elegant flower. So I'm invited back then." She laughed and said, "As often as you like, my dear. You amuse me and I hope I amuse you. And Mrs. Fuller is a great supporter of yours: she says you're a very shrewd housekeeper and not afraid to ask for advice when you need it."

I thanked her, feeling pleased, and went home to convey her message to Margot. She looked at me incredulously. "You called on Lady Tansham and she received you in the drawing room? My dear, I know of several people in the neighborhood who would kill to get invited to that drawing room." I laughed. "I had a recommendation from Mrs. Fuller," I said. "She's Mrs. MacDonald's sister and she put me on to Mrs. Stockton and Mrs. MacDonald for our household. I went to the back door to find out about servants and Mrs. Fuller told me to come to the front door next time because Lady Tansham likes redheads." I don't think Margot entirely believed me until Violet Tansham duly appeared at our door on Thursday.

In a few days we got the reply-paid telegram from Robin saying that she could come the next weekend--from Friday to Sunday. I walked to the station to meet her on Friday. We embraced and I asked her if she had any trouble getting to the station in London. "No," she said, "I got the tu'penny tube right to Paddington. You'll have to try it next time you come to London: it goes within a few blocks of our house. Mother would love to have you stay with us: she's a 'periodic' drunk and she's not on a bender now. Oh, by the way, I discovered what's wrong with Mrs. Varley. She's a secret drinker; never quite sober and never quite drunk during the day." I looked at her incredulously. "Believe me, Vicky, I know all about drinkers, from living with my mother," she said. "All of her friends now are drinkers of one kind or another. You'd never have gotten away with half of your money making schemes if there was a good housekeeper there."

"I don't suppose I would" I said. "Shall we take a cab to Aunt Margot's or do you want to walk?" She said "Let's walk: I'll get to know Oxford better that way. All I've got is this old carpet bag." I agreed, "All right, but let me carry it first. How are things going at my other aunt's house?" She laughed. "I've improved on your money making schemes. Remember how the laundry was often late and how they lost things? Now I take the laundry home with me at the end of the day and one of our neighbors does it. I give her a fair share and keep the rest. And I've got your cook a better price for her table scraps and grease by taking them to my neighborhood. How about you?"

"Aunt Margot lets me take complete charge of the household" I told her. "I hired the cook, Mrs. MacDonald, and the heavy cleaning woman. I do some of the light cleaning myself and Margot does the rest. We've cut out a lot of what housemaids usually do: for example, you're welcome to have a fire in your room, but you'll have to carry up the coal yourself, and if you want a fire in the morning, you'll have to lay it out the night before. I do that , and when I wake up I go over and light it and then snuggle in bed until the room gets warm. I'd do it for Margot at the same time, but she's from an older generation: she feels virtuous getting up and dressing in an icy cold room, and only then going down for breakfast. Sometimes I surprise her by bringing her tea in bed and starting a fire for her, but she regards that as pure indulgence."

Robin looked at me consideringly. "You call her Margot, and you like to do things for her. You're not in opposition to her, as you were with Aunt Maddie, and to some extent with Aunt Ceal? You don't try to make any money out of her as you did with them?" I shook my head, "She'd give me anything she has and I'd give her anything I have. When I expressed a desire to have you visit, she was the one who suggested the telegram. By the way, do you want to share my room, or would you rather have a bedroom to yourself?"

"That telegram increased our standing all over the neighborhood" said Robin. "I'd like to share your room, if you don't mind. We can talk and talk." But perhaps that turned out to not be such a good idea. After a pleasant meal with Aunt Margot, we retreated to my bedroom, where we unpacked Robin's carpet bag, and she looked over my dresses, most of which she'd seen. Then she caught sight of my seal ring. "Now that's new" she said. "Where did you get that?" I said slowly "I guess it's really a loan. It belongs to Mr. Arthur Evans, Keeper of the Ashmolean Museum here in Oxford. He sent it to my uncle with some other things from his digging in Crete--that's near Greece, you know. I got the ring out of a box Mr. Evans sent to my uncle and I suppose that eventually I'll have to give it back."

Robin looked at the design closely: she was the first person who had done so. "A half naked woman on some kind of mythical beast. You'd better not let your Aunt Maddie see *that*" she said. I hesitated, then plunged in. "Robin, there's a story connected with the ring. Let me tell you all about it before you say anything." I poured out the story of my experiences in Crete: she listened without comment, but then she said "And you say this wasn't a dream? You were really there?" I looked at her earnestly. "I know it sounds fantastic, Robin, but it really happened."

She looked at me with an expression I couldn't read and then burst out. "Leaping over bulls! Consorting with a princess! Making friends with people, who if they existed would have been dead for almost three thousand years! Victoria, you're either insane, or trying to pull my leg. In either case, I don't want to sleep in the same room with you! I'll take that other bedroom, thank you." She snatched up her carpet bag and some armfuls of clothing and stalked out, leaving me dumbstruck.

Chapter Five

I woke up in the morning with a heavy heart and got out of bed to light the fire. But instead of snuggling back in my warm bed, I sat cross legged by the fire, looking at the flames. I had never thought that Robin would doubt me. Then I heard the door open behind me and Robin's voice saying "I'm sorry, Vicky, for saying I didn't believe you. Is that the way you dressed in Crete?" I looked down at my only garment, an old petticoat which I had chopped of with scissors to about the length of a kilt. "More or less," I said. "Ever since it happened I've been bothered by all the clothing we wear nowadays. I can't sleep in even a simple shift, much less the heavy nightgowns with all their decoration that women wear today. Of course it's a lot warmer in Crete."

"I'm sorry I flew out at you," Robin said. "It wasn't the bull leaping or the princess: it was how you described your friendship with Helena and the others. I've always been your only real friend and now you have Helena and the others. I suppose I was just jealous." I turned and hugged her. "You're still my only *living* friend, Robin, and my first friend." Robin shook her head. "You're also friends with your Aunt Margot: I was a little jealous of that before you told me your story. I guess I'll have to settle for being your first friend and the only living friend your own age. And that's silly of me because I've made a new friend, too. Can I tell you about it."

"Of course," I said, steeling my heart against a reaction like Robin's. Men say friendship doesn't involve jealousy, but if that's true it may be true only of men. "It all started with me going to the bank for the weekly expenses, just as you used to do. There was a lady there--well she turned out to be a rather high-class lady's maid and companion. Her name was Dominique, and though her English was good there were gaps in it. She was trying to explain something to the bank clerk and she didn't know the English for it. I'd learned a fair amount of French from Solange and I was able to help her. We had tea together after doing our business at the bank and she asked me to meet her mistress. I might have hesitated if I had been carrying the household expenses, but I had just gone to the bank to take a note from your Aunt Stone to the bank manager. So I thought, what could I lose: two women weren't much of a danger to a tough young bird like me, and the address Dominique wanted me to go to was a very good one--in Knightsbridge, on Cadogan Square."

"Dominique is a nice girl, but it's her mistress who's become my new friend. When we got to the address it turned out to be a whole house--not just an apartment. It was absolutely gorgeous and the lady was gorgeous, too. She's a red head, too, but her hair is not as red as yours, more a dark red. Her name is Lillie Langtry and she's an actress. Her husband is an aristocrat, but he has very little money, and he ran up all kinds of debt. Lillie had to go back to acting to make some money."

"She wanted me to coach her on how to speak with a cockney accent: she's looking at a play that requires her to do that. She says real cockneys are no help to her because somehow they don't hear their own accent.

I'd mentioned to Dominique that you and I used to put on cockney accents when we wandered around the city. Lillie said I was a perfect coach because I spoke like a lady, but knew how to speak like a cockney and I could teach her how I did it. Oh, and Vicky, she's such a fascinating person. She's not only an actress, but she's a friend of the king! A *very good* friend!"

I looked at Robin. "Do you mean..." I said. "I'm afraid so," said Robin. "She was his mistress, but she didn't seem to be a *bad* woman, just very ...unconventional. She calls him Berty." I said slowly, "If you'd told me that when I was living at Aunt Maddie's I would have been quite shocked. But after my experience in Crete I'm not so sure what makes a bad person. Minos, the king of Crete, was, I think, a bad man. And his daughter, Ariadne, was doing everything she could to frustrate his plans. You know what Aunt Maddie would say about a daughter who defied her father. But Ariadne was a good person, better than Helena or me, or even Alceme. And I'm really very confused about the relations between men and women. I don't know what's good or bad, except that I don't want the kind of marriage I've seen around me where the man is master and his wife is a slave--the kind of marriage that Aunt Maddie pretends to believe in."

"I think that she really does approve of most women being slaves to men, except for a few matriarchs like herself, and everyone ought to obey *them*," said Robin. I nodded: that was a very shrewd observation on Robin's part. Suddenly I burst out, "Is this Lillie

Langtry prettier that I am?" I immediately felt like a fool for asking.

Robin smiled tenderly. "She's different from you," she said. "You're young and beautiful and almost everyone likes you. She's mysterious and sophisticated and men go mad for her. In ten years you might be very like her if your life goes that way, but if she saw you kneeling there by he fire, half naked and with no cosmetics, she'd envy you, Vicky." "She uses cosmetics, then," I said, feeling somehow lighter hearted.

"She uses them so well that no man could tell, but a woman can tell if she uses her eyes," said Robin. "I'd like to have a few lessons from her. I'm not a natural beauty like you, but well made up and well dressed I think I could be...interesting." I looked at her in horrified fascination. "You're not thinking of following her line of work, either on the stage or in..." Robin shook her head. "Even if I wanted to, I'd need a lot more experience," she said. "I don't plan to spend my life fooling Aunt Maddie and cozening Aunt Ceal."

I looked at her. "If you're unhappy there, for heaven's sake, don't stay," I said. She shook her head. "It's the best way for me now to take care of Mother. If she got better or...died, that would be another thing. Besides, I'm still at the stage of enjoying my cleverness in getting money out of Miss Stone. You were at that stage for a while, but not long before the General came to your rescue, you were sick of it: I could tell." I nodded. "Yes, I was. Let's hope someone will help you get out of your situation."

"Maybe I've already met the person who can help me," said Robin. "But Vicky, I haven't told you the best part. I told her about our friendship and Lillie Langtry wants to meet you!"

I didn't meet Lillie Langtry for a while, but other people who knew one of us wanted to meet the other. Margot was charmed with Robin, and word of our weekend guest got to Lady Tavisham through the servants. An invitation for all three of us for tea on Sunday was carried over to us by Edie. Margot told me, "Make my excuses, Vicky. Violet and I have known each other a long time: she's really interested in seeing what Robin is like. She's got a lot of curiosity, but mainly about people. Petty used to say that if she had that much curiosity about an academic subject, she could have been a fine scholar."

When we arrived for tea, I made excuses for Margot, but Violet snorted, "Next time I issue an invitation including her, make her come. She's shut herself up too much since Pettigrew died. Oh, well, I suppose I'll have to make an effort and call on her. Now I'm going to have a sherry and I know Victoria would like one, too. How about you, Miss Armitage?" Robin declined in a colorless voice. "Against it on principle?" she asked. Robin shook her head: "I'm against it for me," she said. "I've seen its bad effects on people close to me."

Lady Violet nodded. "Quite right, my dear," she said. "Some people need to be careful about getting started on drinking--it runs away with them--but Victoria and I are moderate drinkers, aren't we, Vicky?" I laughed. "I hope so," I said, but I looked a little anxiously at Robin: I wondered if her friendships with me--or Mrs. Langtry--were putting temptation in her way. Robin was much more subdued with Violet than she had been with Margot, and on our way home I asked her if she was overly impressed by Violet's title. "No," she said, "It's that her eyes seem to see right through you and know all your secrets. I felt sure she knew all about Mother just from looking at me.

But when I saw Lady Violet after Robin had left for home, she said, "Her father was Ronny Armitage, wasn't he? Charming man, but drank his way through his inheritance. I don't blame her for shunning drink." I searched my memory. "I think her father's name was Ronald, but I know he died when she was quite young." Violet nodded. "And so her mother is too much against drink or else she learned how to drink from Ronny. No, I know it's none of my business, Vicky. I wouldn't question you about your friend's problems." But I feared that my too expressive face had already answered her question.

A short time later, Margot said to me, "I've heard that Mr. Evans is back in town from his excavations. I think you'd better take that box back to him and see if he wants the contents." Mr. Evans lived outside of Oxford in an area called Boar's Hill, so I had to hire a carriage to take me there. The door was opened by a pleasant-faced woman who, when I asked to see Mr. Evans, brought me into a side room and asked me to wait. After a little while, a man dressed in a Scottish kilt came in. "I'm Duncan MacKenzie, Mr. Evans' assistant, Miss Marsden. If you've come about the job, I'm afraid it's already filled." I looked at him, surprised. "No, it isn't about a job: I have some things that Mr. Evans sent to my uncle, Professor Pettigrew, and my Aunt Margot sent me to see if he wants them back." The man stared at me for a moment. "Good heavens, you must be Victor Marsden's daughter! I'm pleased to meet you, and please accept my sympathy for your sad loss of your parents. Wait a minute and I'll get Mr. Evans."

He came back in a moment with a small man who looked active and energetic. He was just stuffing a pair of spectacles into his pocket, and I recalled what Margot had said about his problems with seeing. The Scotsman said, "This is Elizabeth and Victor Marsden's daughter. She's living with Margot Pettigrew now." Arthur Evans gave my hand a vigorous shake. "Pleased to meet you, my dear," he said. "I only met your parents a few times, but my late wife and I were very fond of them. Margaret and I met the Schliemans when he was excavating Troy and Mycenae, and it turned our interests almost completely to archeology. My late wife and I had hopes of having the same effect on your parents, but then their yacht sank. How I could have used them at Knossos."

I almost burst out crying. "Oh, Mr. Evans, it's so wonderful to meet a friend of my parents. Up until a short time ago I was staying with my mother's sisters, the Misses Stone, and they completely discouraged any talk about my parents..." Mr. Evans patted my hand. "Now, now," he said. "I am very pleased to meet you. Please allow me to be your honorary uncle: no more Mr. Evans, Uncle Arthur will be excellent. Now what's this about a package I sent to Pettigrew?"

The Gryphon Seal

he went on, trying, I think, to move the topic to one less emotionally loaded.

"Here it is: it arrived just before Uncle Pettigrew's death. I don't think he had time to look at it." He sorted rapidly through the contents. "Hm--nice cup but we have a carload of them. Ah, that piece of fresco I sent Pettigrew, I can use that to help reassemble the fresco..." I said hesitatingly, "Mr. Evans--Uncle Arthur, there was something else in the box that I've gotten rather fond of..." I held out my hand with the seal ring. Arthur Evans held it up very close to his eyes. "Very nice ring. Hm, you don't want to show that design to the local Mrs. Grundies. We don't have quite a carload of rings of this quality, but we have plenty of them. Take it with my blessing, my dear, in memory of your parents."

Seeing the tears come to my eyes, he went on swiftly, "Do you know that signets like this led me to Knossos? Not rings usually, but the kind that hung on a cord around your neck or wrist. Saw some of them in a shop in Athens. Told me they came from Crete. Went to Candia, tried to find more. Plenty of them, but nursing mothers had them around their necks. Wouldn't give them up--said they brought out the milk for nursing--called them milk stones." An expression of slight discomfort passed across Mr. MacKenzie's face and Arthur said to him, "Nonsense, she's not a prude or she wouldn't be wearing that ring. Take a look at that design. But they said you could dig them up at Knossos, not far from Candia. Went out and dug and found myself a whole new civilization!"

The assistant took my hand gently and looked at the ring. "I can see you have interests in common with Mr. Evans. Sir, I have to see to the unpacking. You go on telling Miss Victoria about your discoveries." He moved quietly out of the room. Arthur Evans looked after him. "My late wife, Margaret, was quite a scholar herself, you know. Her father was Freeman, the historian. Served as his secretary and assistant for years, just as Duncan does for me. Margaret had an immense knowledge of history: proficient linguist, too; spoke modern languages better than I do. What are we doing in here? Come on into the study, I'll show you some things. Oh, Polly put you here because she thought you'd come about the job."

"I wish I had, though. Your Mr. MacKenzie said it was already filled," I told him. "Working here in any capacity would be so interesting. But I've got practically a full time job looking after Aunt Margot." Arthur Evans said, "Well, the young lady I've hired has family obligations herself and can't come as often as I'd like. May be able to work the two of you each part time. At the moment, it's mainly unloading packing cases and checking the numbers against a list."

"That would be wonderful," I said. "I'm sure we can work something out." We stepped into a crowded study, and the first thing that caught my eye was a bull's head on a little stand; definitely a jumping bull. But a photograph on the table drew me over. It was a picture of a reconstructed fresco and the theme was quite a familiar one. "These are Leapers," I said. "The boy is doing a head leap; one girl is about to do one too, and the other girl is the catcher." Arthur looked

The Gryphon Seal

at me in astonishment. "You must have seen some of the research reports I sent to Petty, or else your father wrote to you about what he'd seen when he visited the site. Yes, that's my theory too. They're leaping the bull, both boys and girls. Went to Spain and asked some 'bullfighters'. Said it was impossible, but I'm sure they're wrong."

Oh, they're wrong, all right," I said, half to myself. "It's difficult, but not impossible." Arthur struck the table with his fist. "That's what I want in this work, someone with imagination. The young men don't have it: all they're concerned with is getting a 'good' degree, and not being considered wild men like certain people in this room. What do you think about my idea that Crete was originally a matriarchy?" "Well, it once was, but seamen came and intermarried, and men got to have a more equal share. But, of course, the husband of Ariadne would be the next Minos." He leaned forward eagerly. "My theory exactly. 'Minos' was a title, like 'Pharaoh' in Egypt. I hadn't thought of Ariadne as being a similar title, but it makes sense. Perhaps I ought to come and work for you!" I looked at Arthur Evans with some concern: by simply stating what I knew to be the facts about ancient Crete, I had confirmed his very acute theories, and earned myself a reputation for originality simply by stating the facts as I knew them.

Chapter Six

Uncle Arthur, as I was beginning to think of him, eyed me keenly and said, "And what do you have to say to my Spanish bullfighters. They said that a bull would never let a man jump over his back, that the bull-leapers would be gored and trampled." I spoke slowly, restraining myself from simply telling him, trying to put it as a suggestion or theory. "Well, there are people who are very good with animals; some people call them 'beast-wizards'. Suppose the Leapers had something like that who could control the bull. That and constant training..." He laughed boisterously. "I'm really tempted to agree with you in private, but if I put that theory in a paper people would be sure that I was a 'wild man'. I think I misspoke myself a moment ago: both of the people in this study would be classified as 'wild men' by most of my colleagues here at Oxford and other places."

"Have you been to the Ashmolean Museum yet?" he asked. "I've really improved it. I even paid for a new heating system so the exhibits could be preserved at an even temperature without fires all over the building." I shook my head. "I haven't really had a chance yet. I've been trying to make life easier for Aunt Margot. We've got good servants now and I'm trying to feed her up, but she still gets very tired much too easily." He looked at me with a keen expression. "If I know Margot Pettigrew, you must have hired the servants: she and Pettigrew didn't have much practical sense between them and Pettigrew had most of it. Did you ever meet him? He was a fine man." I shook my head. "No, I didn't, much to my regret. I wonder, does the firm who did changes on the museum do private houses? Our whole gas system is really unsafe, and I'm going to see if Uncle Sylvester might authorize a complete redo of it. He handles my father's estate, and I'm sure he'd look into Margot's affairs, too."

He nodded. "I think the address of the firm who renovated the museum's heating system is in my files. I'll write you a letter of introduction to them, and also a note to the museum staff to treat you and Margot as honored guests. Your father and Petty gave contributions to our excavations in Crete: you certainly deserve special treatment."

"Thank you, Uncle Arthur," I said. "You have been so kind to me--I really do appreciate it." He shook his head. "I have a feeling that you've been very kind to poor Margot: I'd have done more myself if we hadn't been in Crete. What you want in that house is central heating. Once it's installed you can take care of it easily: you can hire a man to come in and take care of it periodically and the company will send someone out if you have problems. Make sure you have heated towel rails in the bathroom." I laughed. "The motive for the whole thing is to get me a really good bath. We have a geyser..." He shook his head. "I know, aren't they the limit."

I left the Evans house well fed and stocked with information, and the box I had brought with me refilled with Cretan artifacts which Uncle Arthur had plucked from his shelves, saying that they had more things from this trip to replace them. I had notes, written on black edged stationary (a sign of mourning for his wife), to the heating firm and to the museum staff. Best of all, the ring was now mine. But I needed Uncle Vester's approval before I could go ahead with renovation so I wrote him.

In a few days he came down in his carriage, and after chatting with Aunt Margot asked to see me alone. "Do I have money enough for this renovation?" I asked him. "Yes, you do, my dear. Your father was a fairly wealthy man--ran his own yacht, which is more than I'd like to handle myself. But your Aunt Margot has very little money: are you proposing to make this renovation as a gift to her?" I nodded. "Yes," I said, "after all, I live here too, and it will make things so much easier. In the spring we'll have to have a gardener and we can get someone who knows how to deal with the heating system."

"One of the things that kept your father's estate in such a mess is that your Aunt Stone simply handed it over to some very conservative lawyers who didn't use it to make any money. Granted, it didn't lose any either. Know the parable of the talents?" I laughed. "You mean that those lawyers were like the servant who put his talent into a napkin and the king asked him why he didn't put it with the bankers to get interest?" He laughed. "Exactly so. Our blessed lord knew people and how things worked. I more or less, asked the lawyers the same thing. By the way, your Aunt Maddie didn't profit from your inheritance: she hates to spend money but she's honest in her own way."

"Well, good for her," I said a little acidly. "If I have enough, I might want to make a contribution to the Ashmolean Museum." He shook his head. "Arthur

Evans' father is coining money with his paper factory and the Ashmolean is Arthur's private hobby. You save your money for enterprises which really need it: I can suggest some." I said thoughtfully, "He didn't seem to live like a rich man: the house was large, but didn't seem to be luxurious."

"That's probably going to change," said Uncle Vester. "John Evans, Arthur's father, is not in the best of health, and Arthur will get his fortune with no strings attached. It won't be long before he gets a knighthood, and be Sir Arthur Evans. But anyway, the Ashmolean will never lack for anything it needs as long as Arthur is its Keeper. I've also heard that they're thinking of making him an honorary professor of archeology at Oxford." I smiled. "I'm sure he deserves it. I'd like to do something to help Crete, if not the museum." He laughed. "Got the Cretan bug, eh? Evans will know. He owns the site at Knossos, but he was only allowed to buy it for services rendered to Crete. Well, see your heating people and tell them to send me the bill: I'll probably have to sell some of your less profitable shares. If you want to conceal what you're doing from Margot, which I have an idea you do, you can give me the credit as head of the family." I smiled. "Yes, I'd like you to take credit: I don't know if Margot would accept it if she knew I was paying for it."

I saw the heating contractors the next day and set up a complete renovation of our gas system with gas fires and heating and some kind of safety devices on the gas lamps. Oxford had no company to generate electricity for the public, though a few buildings had their own electric power, or I would have chosen to electrify the house. That evening, after Margot had gone to bed, I unpacked the box of presents Arthur Evans had given me. I had an idea that the previous adventure I'd had in Crete was due to the combination of my seal ring and the previous batch of artifacts. I think I might have been holding onto the piece of fresco when the lights went out. This time I picked up a little statue of a bull and waited quietly.

There seemed to be a mist in the room concealing its outlines, and gradually a smoky tunnel appeared in the mist. This was what I expected from things people had told me on my previous adventure. I walked down the smoky tunnel. Presently, I saw sunlight ahead and stepped out in bright sunlight onto a what I thought was the dock at Amnisos. A ship seemed to be pulling away from the dock behind me, and in front of me was a short, roundheaded man who looked very much like one of the servants of the Dance. "You're a candidate for this years dancers?" he said. "By what right do you claim a place in the competition?" I looked around and saw Helena further down the dock. She was wearing the normal dress of a lady of the court; a flounced skirt and a jacket which left her breasts bare. She looked a fair amount older than when I had seen her on my last trip, perhaps twenty years or so. I decided to answer the many questions with a lie, and perhaps explain to Helena later

"My mother was a Leaper with Antimodorus' troupe," I said, hoping that I was in the right time period. The bull-handler said, "The red haired girl who had an accident and had to retire. Yes, my father told me about her. If you're any good at the Dance you should easily make the troupe. I don't need identification: you bear your credentials on your head, Lady." He turned to Helena who was coming up to us and said, "Lady, this is..." But she said uncertainly, "Vicky?"

"I think you may be confusing me with my mother," I said, hating to lie to Helena. "Are you Helena? My mother would have wanted me to greet you with her blessing." Helena nodded. "Of course, you must be her daughter; but you look just as I remember your mother. Would have wanted...she's not alive then?" I shook my head. "No, Lady, my mother is dead." That was true and Helena recognized its truth. "What a pity: after her accident she went away so quickly that I didn't have time to bid her farewell. I don't have any children interested in the Dance, all soldiers or sailors or priestesses. So, you'll be my special protégé. Is your name Vicky, too?" I said, "Yes, Lady Helena," and was immediately told to simply call her Helena. She had evidently stayed in Crete, or returned to Crete, because she had the flounced skirt and open jacket of a Cretan noblewoman. Despite her implied claim of at least three children, her exposed breasts were still quite attractive. "Let me take you to the temporary Mistress of the Dance," she said. "She's a sister of the Sea-King, and since we don't have any tauromaths yet, she's organizing things for the time being."

We went up the familiar path to Knossos. The House looked very much the same, though I could see more repaired earthquake damage: Poseidon, the Earthshaker, had evidently been active. The practice court was still in the same place, and in it was a dark haired girl with some resemblance to Ariadne. Helena explained who I was supposed to be and the girl nodded. "I'm M'pha, sister of Ducalion, the Sea King," she said in Greek with a slight unidentifiable accent. "It's because of that that I'm taking charge temporarily. We hope we have a natural tauromath like your mother's friend, Artimodorus, because there's a problem about going down the Path now. My mother is Alceme, and my father, N'suto, turned out to be the secret son of the old Minos of your mother's day. We lived in Caria for a long time, but we were brought up on stories of Leaping and all of us wanted to try it."

Looking at her closely, I could see some resemblance to Alceme, and some to the dark haired sailor Alceme had married. "From the tales I've heard, your mother was quite a woman," I said. M'pha grinned. "She still is: the Gods only know where she's wandering now, but she'll turn up when you least expect her. You and Helena keep me on track: she remembers my mother as a girl and you've no doubt heard tales of her. We don't have this year's tauromath: do you want to try out? Did your mother give you some training?"

"As much as she could," I said. The Tauromath of the previous group of Dancers, Crateas, a shy young man who had let his sister be mistress of the Dance in his year, was quite comfortable with the bull, a vividly marked black and white bull. I did side leaps from each side of the bull, and M'pha said, "You're practically a professional already. We'll have to start you on the head leap as soon as we can." That was one of my hopes in coming back to the Dance; to be a better Leaper than I had been the first time. In our own time, Rudyard Kipling has a poem "Back to the Army

The Gryphon Seal

Again", about a discharged soldier who reenlists under another name; very much my situation.

"You're definitely in the troupe," said M'pha, "so you can start helping me out as soon as you get settled. Helena, would you take her to the House, see she gets one of the better rooms, and explain the difference between what we do now and what happened when you were a Leaper. "Rooms is one difference," I said. "When my mother was a dancer everyone slept in a dormitory." Helena chuckled. "You still do, but there are walls between the bunks, giving you a little more privacy. Would you like the cubicle which corresponds to your mother's bunk?" I nodded. "Very much so," I said. It was very much 'the same again, but different'. After Helena dropped me off and went back to help out with the new recruits, I didn't have to worry about making mistakes about how things were done now, which reflected exactly how things were done on my first visit. For I now regarded this as another visit, which would come to an end sometime: I hoped not as catastrophically as my first visit. I would have hesitated to go down that shadowy path: I had too much to do in my own time. One of my aims in exploring this world again was to, perhaps, learn a little more about ancient Crete, which I might give to Uncle Arthur as speculations. He had a very accurate nose for what would and would not fit in with the body of facts he possessed. If I threw out as speculations the way things were, he could build those into the picture of ancient Crete.

Two of my personal questions were answered: Helena was very much as I had left her despite her age and children. Alceme had, at least, two marvelous children, M'pha, as well as someone who had managed to inherit the throne of Crete. That must mean that he had married the daughter of the next Minos after the one I had known; but who was that? My less urgent questions about Ariadne and the mysterious Chryseis had not been answered but that might come out in time.

We went on for a while using Crateas, the Tauromath of the current dancers, to handle the bull for the novices, but we knew that this was not a permanent solution. For one thing, it was a strain on Crateas: he was a "natural" beast wizard and was not able to draw on the mysterious sources of power that some legendary Tauromaths, like Chryseis had. So handling the bull for the Dances, as well as for the training, was quite a strain on his powers. Furthermore, the tradition of the Dance--and tradition is very important in the Dance--was that each new group of Dancers must have its own Tauromath.

About this time, there was a distraction from our problem: a visit to Crete by Menelaus, the King of Sparta, and more importantly, his wife, Helen. Helen was the oldest daughter of the former King of Sparta, so Menelaus had gotten the throne by marrying her. This was not an unusual arrangement in the Hellenic world, but in Crete, where the current Minos had gained the throne by marrying the oldest daughter of the previous Minos, this seemed quite a normal arrangement, and for them, Helen was equally important as Menelaus, perhaps even more important.

Furthermore, Helen was a famous beauty: some said that she was the most beautiful woman in the world. There were rumors that her father was Zeus, the King of the Olympians, and I had seen enough on my previous visit not to dismiss this out of hand.

During the earlier part of her visit, I hadn't really seen Helen close up: she was surrounded by high officials and admiring crowds of men--and some women, too. But midway through her visit, M'pha spoke to me one day after practice. "Vicky, Helen has asked to have a private conversation with me and any of the other Leapers whom I want to come. Helen knew my mother after she had left the Dance. Would you like to come and meet her?" I said, "Yes, I'd like to very much, but wouldn't I be interfering in a private occasion?"

M'pha shook her head. "No, if she had said she just wanted to talk to me that would be one thing, but she said any other Leapers I'd like to have come and I'd like you. Frankly, I'm a little scared of meeting Helen alone." I took this with a grain of salt,as I had never known M'pha to be frightened of anything. But that she wanted me to come and share this unusual opportunity warmed my heart. "Then, of course, I'll come," I said. We decided to meet Helen in the female Dancers common room, since M'pla's room or mine would be fairly cramped for three people.

When Helen came into the room, I had to surpress a gasp of astonishment. I had seen pictures of famous London beauties and famous actresses, but this was undoubtedly the most beautiful woman I had ever seen. Her hair was blond, her eyes a sparkling blue, and she moved with such grace and poise that it was simply a pleasure to look at her. Her voice, when she spoke, was beautiful, too, a slightly husky voice with a hint of laughter in it. She came straight to M'pha and took her hands. "I'm so pleased to meet you at last, M'pha," she said. "Your mother is a very dear friend of mine. I wish she'd come and visit me more, but when she was in Sparta just before I married Menelaus, she got rather a bad impression of how Spartans treat women. Having been a Leaper here and then the Lady of the house of N'suto in Caria, she didn't like being ignored and relegated to the women's quarters. Menelaus and I are trying to change that, but it's uphill going. And this is another Leaper? When I first met Alceme, I told her how much I envied the Leapers. You're another fire-top, my dear, like Menelaus."

"I find it hard to believe that you'd envy any other woman, my Lady," I said, as she took my hands, too. She shook her head. "My dear, you and M'pha are quite pretty enough to know that just being a 'face and form' can get in the way of any real relationship. Two men have seen beyond the physical beauty and treated me as a person; Theseus, the former King of Athens, and Odysseus, the King of a rocky little island named Ithaca." I blurted out, "What about your husband?" and mentally kicked myself for my foolishness.

Helen looked at me somewhat enigmatically. "That's always a problem with a man you marry: does he love you or only your beauty," she said and turned to M'pha. "When I first met your mother, my dear, I was hidden away in a little town in Attica, where Theseus had hidden me after he kidnapped me from

Sparta to put pressure on my father to not interfere with Athens. You know how beautiful Alceme was, but for traveling she had a way of making up her face to look like an old woman." M'pha grinned. It was impossible to resist this woman's charm or feel awkward in her presence. "She still does that" M'pha said. "On the other hand, she always wears a Dancer's kilt under her outer clothes and rather welcomes an opportunity to strip down to it. There was an incident in the harbor, where the rigging of one of our ships was fouled. She stripped down to her kilt and climbed the mast to clear it. My brother still talks about it, and so did my father when he was alive. I don't know if Vicky or I will have the confidence to do anything like that after we're finished Dancing."

Helen laughed. "I think you might, if the circumstances were right. You're a pretty spectacular pair, the two of you, and I envy you so much, being able to be Leapers. I hope that the three of us will become very good friends."

Chapter Seven

When you are flattered by the most beautiful woman in the world it is bound to have an effect. I think ever since that meeting I've had a better opinion of my own attractiveness than I had before. And it wasn't just flattery: Helen really meant it. It was something like being complimented by Alceme for making a good Leap. She was a great Leaper and if she liked your Leaping it was an accolade. Similarly, having your beauty praised by Helen was also an accolade: she and Alceme were the best in their respective ways, and could praise you without any envious feelings. Somewhat to my surprise, Helen, M'pha, and I did become good friends. She took time off from her official duties to see us and talk with us, and even did a little training with us. "It's too late," she said wistfully on one occasion. "If I'd come here to train after I left Theseus and was in top shape from hunting and running with him, I might have made a Leaper, but it's a young woman's game really. You two are very lucky."

When we had to part at the end of Helen's state visit, I knew a good deal more about her and M'pha, and was much more impressed with both of them. Helen's kidnapping by Theseus was one of her favorite memories. I think that she had fallen in love with her kidnapper and was not entirely over it. M'pha, I found out, had managed her father's sea-trading business, and looked after her younger brother and sister after her father's death when Alceme had gone off in search of healing for her loss. I felt very much like a junior partner in this three-sided friendship, but they were both very good to me.

When Helen met us for the last time before she left, she told us, "Getting to know both of you has made the trip much more worthwhile. There are so few women in Sparta I can really talk to. If either of you can come to Sparta after you've finished with the Dance, I'll welcome you with open arms." We both said we'd be sure to come, but of course I had no idea how long this visit would last, or whether the Gryphon Seal would take me--or let me go--anywhere else except Crete.

Some time after Helen's departure I knocked on M'pla's door and after a brief pause I was told to come in. There was what looked like an old woman in the room, but as I looked more closely at her I recognized her. Without thinking I said, "But...you're Chryseis, from the first Athenian Dancers." She looked at me and said, "And you're Vicky, the Leaper from Artimodorus' troupe. You're not her daughter, *you're her.* And you don't really belong in this time at all. It's not just that you haven't aged since then--there are other explanations for that. But you come from-- another time--I should have seen that when I knew you before, but I was a little...distracted then." I turned to M'pha and said, "She's right. I should have told you long ago: I'm sorry for deceiving you and Helena by pretending to be my own daughter, but it's such a fantastic story..."

M'pha hugged me and said, "Perhaps I'm a little more used to fantastic stories than most people. This is Chryseis--I call her Aunt Brit for her other name, Britomortis. Her mother was the goddess Aphea, and

Aunt Brit is now an Olympian, too. She and Ariadne and Dion--Dionysus, that is--have been friends of our family as long as I can remember. But if you don't belong in this time, how did you get here?" I held up my hand. "Well, it all began with this seal ring with a gryphon on it..."

Chryseis took my hand and looked at it closely. "That's not my seal, though mine has a gryphon on it, too. I wonder who the girl is." She looked at M'pha and said, "This could also be the solution to your problem about a tauromath for your troupe, M'pha. Used properly, this could make the person who uses it a very powerful tauromath. I don't suppose you've ever noticed this before." M'pha shook her head and Chryseis went on, "It's got a binding on it that no one will notice unless Vicky calls attention to it. I could see it, of course, but that's one of my gifts: I always see what's really there. But now I've lived in Olympus for a while, I can see even more than what's there: this is an important ring, with great powers.

M'pha looked at me. "Now I can see why you were so reticent when Helen and I were telling stories about our lives. Presently, I want you to tell me all about where you've come from and what you've done in this time. But our immediate problem--finding a tauromath--is solved: you can be the new tauromath!" I shook my head. "I somehow know that I couldn't do it. But if I loaned the ring to you..." I looked at Chryseis. "Can I do that? And would it work?"

She nodded her head slowly. "Yes. If it weren't for the Paths being closed because of Olympian conflicts, M'pha could walk down the Path and get a seal of her own. She'd be a good tauromath, too. If you loaned it to her, I could show her how to use it. But the ring is a source of great power: do you really want to let it out of your own hands?" I looked at M'pha. "Loaning it, or even giving it, to a friend is something I can do, especially as good a friend as M'pha is." M'pha looked at me anxiously. "But suppose somehow you don't get it back." I looked at her. "I would trust you with anything I have, M'pha."

Chryseis said quietly, "You can do that. M'pha is just what she seems--honest clear through." I opened my mouth to tell her that I didn't need anyone else to tell me that, but I looked into her steady eyes and remembered that she had said, "I can always see things as they are..." and closed my mouth again. I wondered what she could see in me. As if responding to my thought, she said gently, "I see a woman who has been hurt, but it hasn't made her bitter. She has always made friends, and her friends will always help her, and she will always help them. Don't worry about getting back to your own time if you can't use the ring. By looking at it, I can see how it works, and I can get you back to where you began this trip."

I felt a little overawed. "You really are...a goddess," I said. She shook her head. "I'm an Olympian. The Olympians didn't create the world and we don't rule it, but we can do considerable harm to our enemies and considerable good to our friends." I looked at her. "And who are your enemies?" I asked. She hesitated a moment, then said, "It's a bit complicated. There are forces in the world that are evil--enemies of the human race who will try to enslave and destroy every mortal.

We call them the forces of the Dark, or 'those below'. They and their human allies are our enemies. We Olympians, and other forces--the old Gods especially--are on the side of the mortals. We want them to be free and happy. Our mission is to help them, but we can only help. Mortals have to make their own decisions. The battle is between light and dark, and everyone must choose his or her side."

"Who gave you this mission?" I asked. She looked at me. "There is a God behind the gods who gives us this mission. You might know more about that God than I do. There's what's called the Great Divide, beyond which not even Apollo can see. The Great Divide is at the end of the Olympian mission. After that, the God behind the gods will reveal himself in another way to mortals. I think you come from beyond the Great Divide, so you may, as I say, know more about it than I do."

"Perhaps," I said, "But things get complicated. Some people I don't like or trust talk a great deal about God. Its rather put me off religion." Chryseis laughed. "Things haven't changed all that much," she said. "A lot of the worst people in our time use religion as a mask for their own projects and desires. That's the thing about the Dark Forces and their allies: they always try to corrupt anything which is good and innocent." "Yes, I can see that," I said. How often, when Aunt Maddie said, "God wants you to..." she really meant, "I want you to...."

Chryseis stood up. She no longer looked like an old woman. In fact, she had changed very little since I had met her on my previous trip. "I have to get back," she said. "Your problem seems to be solved M'pha." She turned to me. "I think you could learn to be a tauromath," she said. " M'pha needn't keep the ring: you can just lend it to her. In fact, when you were a Leaper on your previous visit, I always thought that you could do better than you did, but it wasn't my business then."

"Thank you," I said, "But I'd be happier if M'pha was the tauromath. My Aunt Maddie, whom I lived with, would never let me have anything to do with animals, and she discouraged me from doing anything involving exercise or sport. This time I'm getting more confident in my physical powers: I can do a head leap now. Maybe, before long, I'll be more comfortable with animals." Chryseis nodded and said to M'pha, "Give Vicky some practice at using her seal on animals: dogs will do to begin with. I'll come back when I can, but this business has all of Olympus in an uproar." Suddenly she vanished, leaving only a few golden spangles dancing in the air.

M'pha laughed. "Rather spectacular, isn't it?" she said. "You have to get used to sudden appearances and disappearances if you have Olympian friends. But before we do anything else, I want to hear about your life in this other time, and how you got the seal, and..." We talked for hours, and M'pha was both fascinated and horrified. "London sounds very interesting, but I like the idea of Oxford: a whole city filled with places of learning. Your Aunt Maddie sounds terrible: I'm glad you got away from her house. But your Aunt Margot sounds a dear. I'm sorry about your parents. I can sympathize a little: only a few years ago my father died in an accident and my mother left home and has never been back, so in some ways I'm an orphan like you. My grandmother was a very strong-willed woman, and I had quite a few battles with her, but she wasn't nearly as bad as your aunt."

"The thing is, you could argue with her," I said. "Alceme left you in charge of the business and the younger children. Aunt Maddie might not be so bad now, since I'm not dependent on her and don't live with her. I could argue with her how." M'pha laughed. "You've grown up quite a bit between your Oxford experience and coming to this time twice. And if I hadn't grown up the way I did, with Olympian friends like Aunt Brit, it would be strange to think that you knew my mother when she wasn't all that much older than we are now. I'll back you against your Aunt Maddie if it does come to an argument."

That argument with Aunt Maddie was to come sooner than I thought. For a while things went very well. I lent M'pha the ring and she made an excellent tauromath, and our troupe, which was filled with young men and women who had volunteered to be Dancers, was much better than Antimodorus's. I enjoyed having M'pha as a new friend and was enjoying some of the privileges of being a popular Dancer. I had some very nice gifts of jewelry from admirers of the Dance. But one day Britomortus appeared in my room, her face concerned.

"I have a kind of message for you," she said. "In your own time a friend of yours needs you urgently: her name means a small bird in your language." I gasped. "Robin! But how can you get a message from my time?" She hesitated. "It has to do with the True Sun... I'll try to explain some other time, but I think you'd better go back as soon as possible. Time plays some strange tricks, especially since it's such a tremendously long stretch from our time to yours. Shall I get the ring from M'pha?"

"No," I said slowly, "You said you could send me back to my own time without the ring. If I go now and take the ring, it would completely disrupt the Dance. I don't want to say goodbye to anyone--even M'pha. It would be too hard on us both. If I have to go, I want to do it now. And I do have to go. Robin was my first friend, and if she needs me I've got to go." Chryseis gave me a quick hug. "As I told you before, you'll always help your friends. Well, I hope that I'm one of your friends and I'll help you. Somehow or other, if you want to return to this time, I'll manage it in some way."

I looked at her. "That helps a lot," I told her. "Tell M'pha that I'll see her again. But who will take my place in the dance--no one is really prepared." Chryseis laughed. "When Academus's wife, Akama, had the title of Ariadne, before she married him and made him the next Minos, someone attacked her and injured her. My friend, Ariadne, she always went by that name instead of her birth name, took her place, giving the illusion that she was Akama. I can do the same thing for a Dance or two, until they prepare someone to take your place. Then I can have a convenient injury, and the new girl can take your place." She laughed. "When Alceme was pregnant with Academus, she used a supposedly sprained wrist to account for her not finishing out her year. Helena took her place" I looked at her. "I've heard that, but Dancers are supposed to remain virgin..." She grinned at me. "Alceme doesn't always obey the rules," she said. "She's a law unto herself. Well, we'd better get you back."

Suddenly, we were in a familiar cloudy tunnel. "Incidentally, your power to travel in time depends on you remaining a virgin. If you fall in love and would rather give up your virginity to the man you love than return here, that's one thing. But if you want to return here--well, you'd better postpone lovemaking."

"Chryseis," I said, "What do you think about ...men and all that." She shook her head. "I'm a poor person to ask," she said. "I've never met a man who... attracted me that way; even Theseus, even Dion, who I met before he met Ariadne. But at the same time, I'm not sure I want to remain a virgin, like my Aunt 'thena. My mother and father had a wonderful marriage. She gave up her immortality to be with him. That's one reason I joined the Olympians. I don't condemn what Alceme did--she was in love with N'suto, and after he came back from the voyage they were married and had a long happy marriage. Look at M'pha: she's a child of that marriage. As for making love to someone you don't love--well, I don't see how a woman can do it."

I nodded. "Yes, really loving a man enough to spend the rest of your life with him is the only reason I can see to make love to him, but I've never met a man whom I could even conceive of loving in that way," I said. "Neither have I," she replied, "But it can happen to either of us. The business about remaining a virgin if you want to travel in time only applies to taking the

Path from time to time. You can enter the Path for other reasons, even if you're married--or not a virgin. Well, you'd better get going. Walk down the Path until you get home. I managed to make this a Path without a turning: it will lead you straight home. But if you get on a Path without me to fix it for you, remember that given a chance of turnings, always go to the right for the future and the left fo the past. I'll see you again, Vicky and you'll see M'pha again, I promise you."

She gave me a brief hug and vanished. I took the Path ahead of me and walked steadily along it. After what seemed like a long time, the misty walls vanished and I found myself in a familiar room with the contents of the box which Uncle Arthur had given me spread out on a table. I was clad in a dressing gown not in my Cretan clothes and I felt fit and happy. But the finger where I had worn the ring felt very naked and I wondered if Chryseis had the power to fulfill her promise to bring me back to the time I was already missing.

Chapter Eight

Aunt Margot opened the door, entered the room and said, "Oh, Vicky, I'm so glad I found you. You weren't in your bed and I thought you might be out on one of your early morning rambles. This just came to the house by some kind of special messenger." She held out a letter which I ripped open, and, of course, I was not surprised to see Robin's familiar handwriting. "Vicky, I need you. Could you come to my house in London? *Please,*" it said. I told Aunt Margot, "Robin needs me in London, Aunt Margot. Can you do without me for a while?"

She looked at me almost indignantly. "Of course I can," she said. "Your friend needs you. I'll visit the General and get the maids to clean out the house. He hates it, so I have to be there or he'll just browbeat the maids into leaving all of his possessions all over that big house, and it's been too long since I've had them do a real spring cleaning. Yes, go to Robin for as long as you like. Maybe the people could come in and renew the gas system while you're gone: I'll ask Grandfather if he can arrange it."

"That's an excellent idea, Aunt Margot," I said. "I'll dress and pack, and when Mrs. Sterling comes in send her for a carriage to take me to the station. I'll get a hansom cab to Robin's when the train gets to London."

I made an early train, took a hansom cab at the other end (something I'd always wanted to do) and arrived at Robin's by early afternoon. She gave a great sigh when she saw me, and clung to me desperately

The Gryphon Seal

for a few moments. "Oh, Vicky, I'm so glad to see you. Come into the kitchen and I'll make a pot of tea and we can talk. I haven't anything else to offer you. Mother is in the hospital and I don't dare to go to your Aunt's."

When we were settled in the kitchen, she poured out her story. "At first things looked so good. Mrs. Varney got caught about her secret drinking. Your Aunt Maddie offered a visitor a glass of sherry and the bottle was full of tea! There was a big uproar, and it developed that Mrs. Varney had been working away at the sherry your grandfather had laid down--very expensive stuff it seems. When she'd finish a case, she'd fill up the bottles with tea and recork them. They found a half empty case in her closet and she was caught red handed with a big glass of sherry on her bed table. She was sent packing, but it turns out that a lot of things are missing from the cupboard she had the keys to, so I suspect she has a little nest- egg tucked away somewhere. Your Aunt asked me to take over her duties temporarily, and, since you'd been doing most of them while you were here and I'd taken over a few more, it was no burden. But I had to stay at the house overnight more and more...and one day Mother came to the door asking for me. She made a scene and collapsed. I got her to the hospital, but I don't dare to go back to the house. She was obviously--well, the worse for liquor."

"I think that might be gotten over," I said thoughtfully. "Either Aunt Maddie didn't recognize the signs of drink in Mrs. Varley, or she just wouldn't admit that she did. I wonder how much Mrs. Varley was paid. If it was little enough, Aunt Maddie's avarice might have persuaded her to ignore any signs of drinking. After all, I did most of the housekeepers work, and when I left, you did. That way she had a sort of token housekeeper--enough to assure others that she ran a conventional household and the real work was done for free. I think I might be able to get Aunt Maddie to make you an official housekeeper and even give you a salary, but it won't be much. What does the doctor say about your mother?"

Robin looked at me unhappily. "They say she shouldn't be left alone," she said. "She's had some kind of stroke and can't look after herself. If I could get a salary from your aunt, I could pay one of our neighbors to look after her, but..." I nodded. "Yes, but do you want to be a housekeeper--an underpaid housekeeper--for my aunt? Is there any other possibility? You said something about your new friend?" She looked at me with a little hope in her eyes. "I've never had the face to ask Lillie--She's really Mrs. deBath: Lillie Langtry is just her acting name. I try to get my nerve up, but then I lose it. She'd like to meet you, though. I've told her so much about you."

I nodded. "I'd like to meet her. And if you don't have the face to ask her yourself, I'll ask her. When can we see her?" Robin looked at me with admiration. "I knew you'd help in some way if you were here," she said. "Right now she isn't in a play and she told me to drop in on her any afternoon." I said firmly, "There's no time like the present. How do we get to her house?" We could have walked, which Robin usually did, but it would have been rather late for an afternoon call, so

I hailed a hansom as soon as we got to a main street. When we arrived at the house, I stared at it: the place was a small mansion. Could an actress afford a place like this?

We were ushered into the drawing room and found Mrs. Langtry, or Mrs. deBath as she actually was, entertaining a young man who seemed hardly out of his teens. "You run off, Shuggie," she said. "This is my friend, Robin, who's brought her friend Victoria to meet me. We have plenty of feminine things to talk about--you'd be bored." The young man gave us a friendly grin and took himself off.

Mrs. Langtry said to Robin, "I said I'd show you the house someday. Let's break the ice by me showing both of you around; then we'll have some tea." She led us through a series of elegantly furnished 'public rooms' to her own room where she opened a series of doors to reveal what seemed like a shop full of gowns. Robin looked at them and made a little noise like a cat. Mrs. Langtry laughed and said, "Dominique's in the next room: would you like to try on some of these? Of course you may and I'll show Victoria some of the rest of the house. We left Robin with her friend Dominique picking over the dresses.

Our next stop was an elegant bathroom tiled in a sot of blue-green tile with little stars of gold decorating them. The bathtub was marble and looked completely luxurious. I made little cat noises. Mrs. Langtry laughed. "Would you like a bath?" she asked. "There are towels on the shelf and when you're done, put on the dressing gown there on the hook. It's one of mine but it's just been washed." I looked at her and made up my mind. "Yes, I will, Mrs. Langtry. I've just come from Oxford, where we're redoing my Aunt Margot's bathroom. I've just come off a train, and I'd love to have a bath in that marble tub."

She laughed. "Call me Lillie: you can't be on formal terms with someone whose bath you've used. And I'll call you Vicky, if I may: Robin usually does. I'll be in the little sitting room next door when you're finished. This should really break the ice." She left the bathroom and I turned on the taps, first inserting a rather elegant plug in the drain. I stripped off my clothes, noting the lovely hot water from one tap mixing with the cold water from the other tap before it came from the faucet, so you could tell by feeling the water as it came out whether it was the right temperature. Making a note to get the same arrangement for our new bathtub, I plunged into the water. A hot bath at the end of training is one of a Dancer's prerogatives: I was a connoisseur of baths and this was a good one.

When I emerged, in Lillie's dressing gown, into the sitting room, she looked up from some sort of account book she was looking over and smiled. "Next time you can spend more time in the bath, Vicky: there's nothing like a leisurely bath. You look perfectly charming in my gown."

"And you and one other woman I've met are the most beautiful people I've ever seen, Lillie," I said. She laughed. "Some other time I'd like to know about this other woman, but for now I want to talk about Robin. She's in some kind of trouble, isn't she?" I sat on a chair near her, drawing up my legs under the dressing gown and sitting cross legged, and poured out

Robin's troubles. Lillie listened without comment, and then said, "Tell me more about your Aunt and yourself so I can make a better judgment."

I told her about my early life and about Aunt Maddie and Aunt Ceal, but nothing about Crete, yet. She nodded slowly and said, "Yes, I remember your father, Victor Marsden: I met him on some social occasions. He was a very handsome and charming man, but totally devoted to your mother. You resemble her quite a bit, Vicky. Before we get to Robin, I want to make some comments on what you've told me. I can understand you hating your Aunt Maddie: I'm sure I'd dislike her, too. But your reaction against her greed and hypocrisy has made you into a very unconventional--delightfully unconventional to my mind-- young woman. Your Aunt Margot sounds a dear: I think Bertie knew Professor Pettigrew. But don't be overly grateful to General Athlone. He left you to your Aunt's mercy for a long time, and only got you out of that house to take care of your Aunt Margot. He's just as selfish as most of the rest of the family."

I sighed. "I suppose you're right, "I said, "But whatever his motives, he did free me from Aunt Maddie and gave me a whole new life." (Two new lives, I thought.) Lillie nodded. "You can be grateful to him as long as you don't overestimate his nobility. I'm not sure he should have encouraged you to redo the heating system in your Aunt Margot's house. He doesn't own it does he?"

"Oh, no," I said. "I made very sure that she owns it, and I live there, too. Before long I'll be able to take a bath in our own house like the one I just had here. I wonder how much a marble tub costs?" She looked at me with friendly eyes. "Not as much as you may think," she said, "And they're very easy to keep up. Another thing you owe your Aunt Maddie is that by forcing you to be an unpaid housekeeper, she made you a very sensible and practical person. I have some very intelligent women among my friends, but they wouldn't know how to order a new heating system."

"I don't think it was part of my Aunt's scheme to educate me," I said dryly. "Lillie, I don't want to pry, but is the Bertie who knew Professor Pettigrew--the king?" She smiled. "If people do want to pry, I simply pretend not to hear, but you're interested in your Uncle Pettigrew, not in prying into Bertie's life or mine. Yes, Bertie is the king now, thank heavens. His mother would never let him have any position worthy of him and that turned him into a bit of a playboy, but he was always interested in a lot of things, like good scholarly works. Now he's probably killing himself trying to do all the things he thinks a king should do. He's one of my oldest and best friends."

"Thank you for telling me," I said. "It increases my admiration for both of you. But now I think we'd better talk about Robin. She can't take all afternoon looking at dresses, can she?" Lillie laughed. "I think dresses mean a little more to her than to you or me. For me they're mainly costumes. When I first entered London society, my brother had just died. I wore a little black dress in mourning for him. When I got invited to parties I still wore it, partly out of loyalty to him and partly because I didn't have anything else to wear. My dear, 'Lillie Langtry in her little black dress' became an absolute rage in society. When I eventually took off mourning, I was well known enough that dressmakers would give me dresses if I discretely dropped their names; not unlike your little games with the tradesmen. But about Robin: I'd be much more able to help her if I didn't have to go on tour to America to make money. This place requires a lot of cash, you know."

"You pay for this place out of your earnings as an actress?" I said in amazement. She nodded. "The United States helps a lot. They 'love a lord'--or a lady-- there. My earnings from American tours and my horse race winnings support that marble bathtub and all its surroundings." I gaped at her. "Horse race winnings?" I asked. She laughed. "One of my admirers gave me some race horses. He died, and his stables wouldn't pay for their keep, so I raced them and won. He was rather a horrible man, as it turned out, but he was an excellent judge of horses and he made me one, too. You don't imaging that Shuggie's income pays for all this, do you?"

I gaped at her. "The young man we met when we first came--he's your husband?" She looked at me challengingly. "You think that he's too young for me?" she asked, "Lillie, dear, he would have been too young for you when you were *my* age," I told her. She laughed. "How shrewd you are, Vicky. Yes, Shuggie was probably a mistake, but when his father dies, I'll be Lady deBath. In my early days in society, I always wanted to be a Lady, and Shuggie can be good fun."

"Better you than me, Lillie." I told her. "Yes, if you have to go away it limits your chances of helping Robin. She just won't accept money from either of us or I would take care of her myself." Lillie gave me a shrewd look. "You'd better discover exactly what you have in your inheritance. Set that old admirer of your mother's on the General to find out what you have and how it's invested. I have some very good financial people looking after my assets. No, if Robin would just accept money, I could help her, probably better than you, but she won't. I thought of hiring her as an actress in my company: she's a good mimic and that's half the battle. I don't always like the younger actresses in our company: to get where they are they have to be-- hardened-- in various ways. When my daughter came on tours with me, I didn't want her associating with them, but that problem solved itself. She's married, and is no longer...with me."

I could sense an inner agony about her when she spoke of her daughter, but that was certainly none of my business, unless she chose to share it. To some effect, she did, for she said quietly, "I rather wish Jeane-Marie were more like you, my dear. She spent a lot of time with my mother, and she picked up a much more conventional attitude towards things. My mother always made an exception for me, but Jeane-Marie didn't." I said simply, "It's always hard for a daughter and a mother when the mother's more well known. If my mother had lived, I might have quarreled with her."

"Bless you, my dear," she said. "When my hair was redder, in my youth, you could have been my daughter: but yes, we might have quarreled. Red heads are notoriously quick-tempered, as well as other things. If you can find something for Robin to do temporarily, which will enable her to support her mother, we can work at a permanent solution. Frankly, if the mother would just die, I could carry Robin off to America with me. But so long as she's alive, Robin will never go." I nodded. "I think I can patch up a truce with Aunt Maddie that would tide us over for a while. I'd better get my clothing on: more 'conventional' people might not understand that bath." Lillie laughed. "If I were inclined that way, I'd find you very tempting, Vicky, but I'm not. Another of my best friends, Oscar Wilde, is a lover of his own sex, but I've never understood that about him."

When we rejoined Robin, she was still in ecstasies about Lillie's dresses. I thought she might do well on the stage, dressing up and imitating people, but she'd never leave her mother. On the way back to her house, I told her that Lillie was quite anxious to help but had to go to America to make money. She nodded. "Knowing she'd like to help makes me feel better. If only I could go with her! But so long as Mother needs help..."

So in the end, I had to interview Aunt Maddie. At first she tried to dominate me, saying it was my duty to return and help run the household. "That's not going to happen, Aunt," I told her. "The General, for whatever motives, wants me to stay with Margot, and our society being what it is, you can't successfully fight him. In some ways, he's as selfish as you are. And you certainly won't make me feel guilty--I'm out from under your roof and I'll never return. Your best chance is to pay Robin a decent salary so she can take care of her mother and also look after your household." Aunt Maddie bristled. "Her mother was here--her behavior was...

quite inappropriate." I shook my head. "Her mother is ill. She needs to be under constant supervision. Pay Robin a reasonable wage and she'll stay with you. If you don't, she'll have to look for other ways to help her mother." I could see Aunt Maddie struggling with her avarice. "Suppose I allow Roberta to bring her mother here--they can have Mrs. Varley's old suite; I could pay Roberta a small sum in addition."

We argued a bit about the "small sum" and at last I agreed. "It's what I pay my cleaning woman, but she doesn't have her mother in the house. Yes, I'll agree on Robin's behalf." She looked at me. "You and Margot have a cleaning woman?" she asked. "Yes, and a cook, too, whom we pay..." and I named the sum and my Aunt closed her eyes in disbelief. "I'm told by a friend," I said, half in malice, "that I owe you for giving me all the jobs you gave me. I'm told it made me a good manager." She snapped, "Not if you pay a cook *that*. But, yes, you did help out here and I'm not unappreciative. You may not have realized how careful we had to be at times." I looked at her in disbelief. She always had the best of things surely.

But now, looking at her dress and accoutraments with an eye trained by wider experience, I wondered if her things were carefully selected and carefully preserved. Maybe she wasn't really avaricious, only careful--perhaps overly careful, at times. I wondered if I could find out how much Aunt Maddie and Aunt Ceal really had. "I'd have appreciated that more if you'd said it while I was here," I said. "Perhaps I should have," she said, "But Roberta is good, too, I'll agree to your terms."

As I left the house I thought that this was the first real argument I'd had with my aunt. And I'd won!

Chapter Nine

When I went back to Oxford with Robin's thanks and blessings, I felt a little odd. Without Aunt Maddie to react against, I didn't quite know who I was. We had reached terms of grudging respect: we would never like each other, but we did respect each other. When I reached the house, I found the work had been done in my absence, including the instructions I had sent by letter to the heating company. A man from the company came the next day to see if I was satisfied, and he mentioned the marble tub. "My cousin, who works in London, says that that actress Lillie Langtry has a tub like that," he said. "Yes," I said, "I heard about that tub." He eyed me a little dubiously. "Some say she's no better than she should be, but my cousin says she's a nice lady. Gave him tickets to one of her plays, and he said she isn't half bad on the stage. Of course, lots of people just go to see her just to speculate about where her jewels come from-- well, nothing to talk about with a young lady like you. I'll tell my boss that you're pleased with the work, Miss, and if you'd tell Mr. Evans you are, it would be good for business." In my own tub that night, I had an even better bath than I'd had in Lillie's tub, and almost as good as in Crete. One thing the tub lacked was a servant girl to pour water over me. I wondered if I could train Mrs. Stockton to do it, but I giggled when I imagined her face.

The next morning, Margot came home and was delighted with the new gas jets and fires. She looked at my marble tub with its "mixing faucets" a little

The Gryphon Seal

more dubiously: she seemed to fear that it was a little too luxurious for us, but when I told her how much I enjoyed it, she immediately said, "If you enjoy it then I'm sure the General will be happy. He says you've already taken years off my age, and he's very grateful to you."

I'd almost forgotten that the General was taking credit for the heating renovation, but I saw an opportunity here. "Aunt Margot, do you think Uncle 'Vester could find out how much Aunt Maddie and Aunt Celia have in their investments? I thought they were merely-- well--overfond of money, but now I wonder if they're actually in want." My aunt wrote to the General and he replied directly to me. "Your aunts have quite a bit of money, but it's invested so conservatively that they get very little from it. I've tried to get them to make more profitable investments, but with no luck. Don't worry, my dear: their investments are so prudent that it will take the fall of the British Empire to make much difference to their income and holdings."

With that off my mind, I was ready for new challenges. One came in a note from Mr. MacKenzie, Uncle Arthur's assistant. "The young lady we hired can work here at the house, but we realize that this is quite a journey for her to go into Oxford. There are some cases of goods from Knossos at the Museum. Some of these have not been properly catalogued, and Mr. Evans trusts you, not only to list the contents but to add new numbers to uncatalogued items and list them. If you will write me here, we can make an appointment at the Museum so that I can show you the routine. Yours faithfully, Duncan MacKenzie."

I did make the appointment at the museum, learned the routine, and two days a week had my run of all kinds of finds from Knossos: some of them very familiar from my experiences, others, especially those having to do with areas I had little contact with on my trips, strange but somehow familiar. Before long, I could tell by merely looking what came from what Mr. Evans was calling the 'Minoan culture' and what came from the later Hellenic period. Once in a while, Uncle Arthur would look in, eye my work benevolently and drift off again. I found from some acquaintances that I made at the Ashmolean that Mr. Evans, the curator, or as they say, the 'Keeper' of the collection, spent very little time at the museum, and that the Board of Visitors was often rather indignant about it.

The other new opportunity came in a note from Lady Tansham, asking me to come to tea to meet her nephew. The nephew, an undergraduate at Oxford, was a lanky, rather vague young man who was a lord in his own right--Lord Mumford, addressed by his aunt as simply Mumford. He was accompanied by his friend, Steven Harter, who turned out to be, in effect, the person who did a great deal of Mumford's work.

While Mumford exchanged family news with his aunt, I talked quietly to Mr. Harter on the other side of the room. "You needn't be so indignant, Miss Marsden," he said. "Mumford is a lord, and if he gets a government appointment there will be civil servants, people like me, who'll do all the real work for him. When I brief him for his tutorials, it is not much different from civil servants briefing a minister for Question Period in the House. Mumford is honest in

The Gryphon Seal

his way--he'll accept instruction and if he doesn't know something, he'll admit it. He'll graduate from Oxford with a 'gentleman's third class degree' and go on to do the same sort of thing the rest of his life. Meanwhile, what he pays me enables me to stay in Oxford, and if I work very hard, I may get a second, or even a first class degree, and go on to teach or be a civil servant." "I still don't think it's fair," I said.

When Mumford eventually deigned to converse with me, I didn't find his conversation very enlivening. When I expressed some mildly unorthodox opinions about politics, and finally convinced him that these were my opinions and that I was not just being provocative, he looked at me with eyes like a shying horse. "Not the opinions of a lady," he said at one point. "Of course..." He lapsed into silence. His aunt eyed him with exasperation. "Vicky is indeed a lady, Mumford, and if she has somewhat different opinions than those empty headed debs you go around with, it doesn't mean she isn't a lady."

When the men were gone, she half apologized for Mumford. "I know he's a fool, my dear, but with a clever woman behind him, he could make his mark. Even, God save us, be a minister." I laughed. "I'm afraid I'd need someone I respect. By the way, a lady I met in London expressed great admiration for King Edward." She accepted this change of topic without protest. "She's quite right , my dear. Queen Victoria was always comparing him to that German prince she married and was disappointed when he didn't, in her view, match up. But Edward has just as many brains as Prince Albert, and twice, no, three times the originality.

And people like him: he's averted some international incidents, even some wars, by his influence on the other rulers. They're already calling him Edward, the Peacemaker. Of course, almost all the royalty in Europe are related: He's Uncle or Cousin Bertie to most of the crowned heads in Europe." Hearing the king's nickname brought back what Lillie had said about him.

"Do you know--or know of-- a lady called Mrs. deBath? She acts under the name of Lillie Langtry?" I asked. Lady Tansham looked at me in horror. "You stay away from the Lillie Langtrys of this world, Vicky. Even admitting talking to her can ruin your reputation. I admit she's a fascinating creature and quite beautiful, but knowing her would be poison to a young lady's reputation. Even her daughter turned against her after she discovered that her father was--well, wasn't Mr. Langtry. Of course, Langtry was a hopeless drunk, and Lillie, Mrs. Langtry, supported him until he died. Then she married the nineteen year old son of Lord deBath, and if his father doesn't cut him out of his will, she'll eventually be Lady deBath and will have to be accepted. But you avoid her like the plague, Vicky."

"Actually, I found young Mr. Harter rather more interesting than Lord Mumford," I said, changing the subject again. Lady Tansham looked thoughtful. "That's not out of the question," she said. "Well born, of course--father was a youngest son who went in for the church: mother a youngest daughter, who alienated her family by marrying a poor clergyman. But not a penny to rub against another: it will be a long time before he can think of marrying. But Stephen's a good boy; Mumford's father wouldn't have entrusted Mumford to him if he weren't."

I left Lady Violet's house with some rather mixed feelings about her attempt at matchmaking. I was sure that her intentions were kindly, but I didn't want to be married off. I was finding my independent life quite interesting and only wished I could somehow combine the life of living in Oxford with the life of a Leaper in Crete. My work for Mr. Evans kept me from any tendency to forget about Crete: it was full of constant reminders of the life I had led. I found my walk from Aunt Margot's house to the Ashmolean enjoyable and good exercise, even if it took me through a couple of rather shady districts.

On one of my trips to the Ashmolean, I passed a rather run-down looking public house and found Lord Mumford being escorted out the door... "Don't want none of your kind here," said the publican, "Get us into trouble, you will." He turned back into the pub, but Mumford eyed me with a gaze blurred by drink. "You're Miss Marsden, "he said, "believe in votes for women, don't you." Suddenly an idea hit him. "Probably believe in free love, too," he said. "Well, how about a little of that?" He lurched toward me and I prepared to take evasive action, but, from across the street a man in a bowler hat came over and addressed Lord Mumford. "Are you a member of this university, sir?" he asked him in a stern tone. Mumford regarded him with blurry eyes. "Mumford," he said, "Lord Ralph Mumford: I'm at the House." The bowler hatted man looked at me. "And who is this young lady?" he asked. Mumford looked a little panicky. "Niece of

Professor Pettigrew. Was escorting her home." The bowler hatted man looked at me. "Good try, ducky," I said in my best cockney accent. "But I ain't up to the part." I looked at the bowler hatted man. "Think the governor of this pub just threw him out," I said. "Making himself a bit objectionable to me." The man nodded to me. "All right, love, " he said. "I'll take care of him. You run along." I gave him a quick smile and slipped off. Serve Mumford right if I got him into a bit of trouble. The bowler hatted man must be one of the university proctors who were responsible for seeing that the undergraduates kept the university regulations.

As I walked along the street, I ran into Stephen Harter, looking worried. I hailed him with the greeting, "Are you a member of this university, sir?" His worried face broke into a smile. "Miss Marsden, I didn't know the proctors were taking in female members. You'd need a bowler hat, and I don't think it would fit on those curls. You haven't seen a proctor, have you? Or Mumford?" I looked a little guilty. "Well, as a matter of fact, I've seen Mumford with a proctor." He gave a groan. "He gave me the slip," he said. "I'm afraid he's been drinking. If he gets sent down, there goes my stipend. I won't be able to continue at Oxford."

"Oh, Lord," I said, "I'm afraid I got him into trouble. I ran into him and he made himself rather objectionable. I'm afraid I told the proctor he'd been thrown out of the pub, and when he said he was escorting me home, I denied it--in my best cockney accent."

He groaned. "He'll be in real trouble, may get sent down. Lying to a proctor is beyond the pale:

You've got to admit what you've done and take your medicine. Luckily his tutor, Michael Reve has a sense of humor. Would you go with me and tell Mr. Reve what happened?" I nodded. "For your sake, not for his," I said. He took me to a side entrance to Christ Church College(nicknamed "the House") and up some stairs to a set of rooms on the first floor. When we knocked, a firm voice told us to come in. Mr. Reve was almost as tall and lanky as Mumford, but there the resemblance stopped. He had the abstracted air of a scholar who lived mostly in his books and his subject, but his eyes were keen and intelligent.

"Sir, this is Miss Victoria Marsden," said Stephen, "She..." Mr. Reve nodded. "Up at Balliol after your father, Miss Marsden. Met him a few times. You resemble your mother quite a bit. Sorry about the accident." I smiled, liking him at once. "I've come to confess a prank I played on Lord Mumford," I said. "We were having a discussion about votes for women. He rather annoyed me and when a proctor challenged him I pretended not to know him, pretended to be a cockney girl. I didn't know it might get him sent down." Mr. Reve regarded me. "Doubt if that's the whole story, but the worst charge against him would be trying to deceive a proctor. Turned out you did the deceiving, but you're outside our powers to punish." I gave him a friendly smile. "Yes, sir," I said, "But I'm sorry."

He nodded to Stephen. "You're his bear leader aren't you? Well, I'll rake him over the coals, may gate him for a while, but I won't send him down. Shame you have to take care of a man like that to stay at the

Varsity. I'll look into a scholarship for you next term. Also a shame that a bright young whippersnapper like you can't be at the University, Miss Marsden. That may change, but I'm afraid not in our time. As for votes for women, I'm all in favor. Think I'll give Mumford a paper on pros and cons of votes for women. What are you doing in Oxford, Miss Marsden?"

"Staying with my Aunt Margot Pettigrew, and doing some work for Mr. Evams, Keeper of the Ashmolean Museum." He nodded. "Good for you," he said. "Stuff Evans has found in Knossos casts a whole new light on classical history. Give him my greetings next time you see him. Slips in and out of Oxford so that his Board of Visitors can't find him with their complaints. Wish I could do that. Nice to meet you, Miss Marsden. Give my greetings to your Aunt Margot."

When we emerged from the rooms, Stephen Harter looked at me in amazement. "Never seen Mr. Reve so amiable, Miss Marsden. You've saved my bacon. If ever I can do anything for you, please call on me." I said, "You'd better take credit for getting Mumford off. To owe it to me would be a final humiliation." (That turned out to be an unwise decision, but I didn't know it at the time.) I did find Uncle Arthur at the museum and passed on Mr. Reve's greetings. He was pleased. "Good man, Reve. Student of my wife's father. Have to drop in on him one day soon. Now, this crate, which I'll open for you, is last minute stuff, dug up just before the dig ended. Start with the last number on the catalogue and list each item with a brief description. Then put the number on the artifact: did Duncan show you how? Good! See you another time,

The Gryphon Seal

my dear. Wouldn't trust anyone else to do it except Duncan."

I enjoyed lifting the artifacts out and labeling them. In some cases I knew what an artifact was; in other cases I was completely baffled. In a few cases I knew that the accepted description was, in fact, wrong, but I had no evidence except my own memory to provide. Toward the bottom of the case I picked up a small jar and felt something rattle in it. I tipped the jar and spilled out onto my hand--my gryphon seal ring! I knew it was my ring: the whole point of a seal ring was that it must be unique. I could even see a little mark I had made on it in leaping a bull and scraping it on the horn. So, the ring had been in a previous case of artifacts from which I had taken it and I had carried it back to the past where at some time it had been put in the jar and in the present era dug up at Knossos. That meant that there were two rings in our time: one in the box Uncle Arthur had sent to Uncle Pettigrew, and one in Crete waiting to be dug up. For a while, the two rings had been fairly close to each other in Oxford. Probably at some point in ancient Crete there had been two of the same ring. I gave it up. Somehow, my ring, presumably after M'pha was through using it, had found its way back to me, and that meant that it was in someone's--or Someone's--plans that I would make my way back to ancient Crete. There was no hurry, now: I knew I could do it.

After my work at the museum, I took my usual route home. As I went through one of the shady districts, I heard a voice behind me. "There she is. Little bitch almost got me sent down! Get her boys, worry her!"

I whirled around and saw Mumford, evidently drunk again, accompanied by a rather loutish man. And racing toward me were two large black hunting dogs!

Chapter Ten

I had always been frightened of dogs, especially black ones. I think, perhaps before I could remember, I had been attacked or at least frightened by a black dog. But Chryseis' little bit of casual kindness, "Teach her how to use the ring on animals--dogs will do to start with," had led M'pha to put me through a series of drills. Fighting down panic, I reached out for the minds of the dogs. They really weren't all that fierce: the command to "worry me" might have led to some nips and rough pushing. They wouldn't really have killed me, but I could imagine most women being sent into an absolute panic by such an attack and ending up in hysterics or a fainting spell.

I got hold of the dog's minds and with a familiar effort made them wheel around and go the other way. It was very much the same thing a tauromath did to a bull at the end of its run. The two men looked with utter disbelief as the dogs raced toward them, then their nerve broke and they ran away as fast as they could. I sent the dogs after them with the same orders in their minds, "worry them," then I turned away.

An old man with a heavy stick in his hand came out from a door nearby. "I was coming to help, Missy, but I don't move as fast as I used to. If you can make animals obey you like that, I'll get you top money in any circus or show you like." I laughed. "I don't plan to make it a profession, but thank you. And thank you for coming to help." He grinned. "Keep it in mind, lady. I'm always here or hereabouts. Abel's my name:

they call me Gypsy Abel. I know a beast wizard when I see one, and you're the best I've seen."

"I will keep it I mind," I said, "but I have responsibilities to an aunt who isn't in very good health. So, thank you, Mr. Abel, and if I ever want to run away to the circus I'll remember what you said." He grinned. "Oh, it's a good life, missy," he said. "But I understand taking care of relatives: my old dad needs a lot of looking after: that's why I'm staying in Oxford for a while. I don't suppose your aunt would come with you?" I laughed. "She might have the spirit, but not the strength," I said. "I hope we meet again, Mr. Abel." He shook his head. "Gypsy is good enough for me," he said. "Don't worry about not being treated like a lady if you were in a circus or show. With your talent, you'd be at the top of the bill, and such people are treated with respect." I smiled at him. "My name is Victoria Marsden, and I really do hope we meet again."

Walking back to our house, I pondered how my experiences in ancient Crete might affect my future life. I could envision being in a circus or show: it was not all that different from being a Leaper. I certainly didn't want to spend my life as my Aunt Maddie and Aunt Ceal did where the great excitement of the day was making a formal visit to the house of people whom Aunt Maddie regarded as her social equals, or receiving a visit from them. I'd like a bit of excitement in my life, traveling, perhaps, or learning something worthwhile.

An opportunity to do just this was waiting for me when I reached home. Aunt Margot called to me as I came in. "Vicky, there are some callers here for you, Miss King, who is a student at Somerville College and her friend Miss Pankhurst, visiting from Manchester. I'll go see to the tea and you can make friends while I'm gone."

After Aunt Margot left the room, the older girl, Miss Pankhurst, spoke in a low urgent tone. "The reason we're here, Miss Marsden, is perhaps best talked about while your aunt is out of the room. Word has reached us that you're in favor of votes for women. Is that so?" I nodded. "Yes, I definitely am. My mother left me Mrs. Wollestonecroft's *Vindication of the Rights of Women* and I'm quite convinced by her arguments," I said. Miss Pankhurst said, "My mother, after my father died, founded the Women's Social and Political Union. We're in the forefront of the struggle to get votes for women, and Mrs. Wollestonecroft is an honored hero of our society." I liked this rather intense young woman, but I had some objections. "Surely there are an awful lot of things which women can do for themselves or each other without having the vote," I said.

Miss Pankhurst nodded. "Of course there are, and we're in favor of them all. But to accomplish anything fundamental, women have to have the vote. We're very much against child labor and very much in favor of wealthier women helping poorer women, for example, but if you write to your member of parliament about these issues, most M.P.s simply throw your letters away. Since women have no vote, the politicians can safely ignore them."

I frowned. "Yes, that does make me angry. If there's something which is unjust it shouldn't matter who brings it up." I remembered both Ariadne and M'pha spending a fair amount of time talking to people with grievances, and using their influence to get wrongs righted. Of course, in ancient Crete women were respected and honored. Miss Pankhurst replied, "I can see that you'd be an outstanding recruit to our ranks, but our immediate problem is Dorothy King. She really needs someone to support her." Miss King blushed. "I can stick it out alone," she said, "but it would so help to have someone sympathetic to talk to, as Christobel says"

"Well, I can certainly do that," I said. "But you're at one of the colleges; don't you have any support from your fellow students, or the teachers?" Dorothy shook her head. "Women's colleges, like Somerville, are just one stage up from a finishing school," she said, "When we go to lectures in the University, we're always accompanied by chaperones--nice old ladies who sit and knit while we listen to the lectures." She went on slowly, "Some of the women are there because it makes them more marriageable to men who've been at the Varsity, and some who really want to learn are very leery about getting involved in politics. There are a lot of jokes about us suffragettes and quite a bit of hostility to us. Many women at Somerville are looking forward to teaching at girl's schools or even at Somerville. They don't want to get involved in anything as controversial as 'Votes for Women'."

I looked at her a little more closely. It was a shrewd observation, and there might be more to this girl than appeared on the surface. "What about you?" I asked. She blushed again. "I come from Manchester, too," she said. "My father got rich from selling wool. I'll have plenty of men after me for my father's fortune, but if I don't choose to marry I won't have to get a teaching job."

"Yes," I said thoughtfully. "I have some money from my father, too. You want to make very sure that men want you and not your money." I caught an interested glance from Christobel Pankhurst: probably, like many with a 'cause' she was on the lookout for contributions. Well, that might be all right, but I'd learn more about the Women's Social and Political Union from Dorothy and if I liked what I heard, I might very well give them a contribution. Christobel turned to Dorothy. "I have some other appointments in Oxford, Dorothy," she said, "and I know I'm leaving you in good hands. Make my excuses to your aunt, Miss Marsden, and tell her I have to meet some people. Whether you tell her about the WSPU I'll leave up to you." She rose, shook hands with me and strode out of the room.

Dorothy looked after her with her eyes full of admiration. "Isn't she splendid?" she said. "I'd like so much to be like her." I said thoughtfully, "I've known a few women like her. I think 'Votes for Women' is more important to her than any individual person; but yes, she is rather splendid in her way."

Dorothy said, "I know what you mean. I do have a bit of a pash for her, but I think that's better than some of my fellow students falling for every handsome don who lectures at the University. I don't really think I'm a Lesbian" She reddened again and gave me a beseeching look. I took the comment more calmly than most of her contemporaries would have. "I don't think that admiring, or even loving a woman makes you a Lesbian. There are some women that I love and admire very much." Ariadne, for instance, and Chryseis, and even M'pha, though my feelings for her were a little different; she didn't overawe me as the other two did. About Helen and Lillie Langtry, I had rather mixed feelings.

Dorothy nodded. "Yes, I think it's important for a young woman to have some female ideals, and in some ways Christobel is one of mine. I think women need living women as ideals, not dead people whom you can't get to know, such as my mother who died ten years ago, or Our Lady."

'Our Lady?" I asked. "You mean the Mother?" She nodded. "Yes, Mary, the mother of Jesus. Our family is Roman Catholic and most Protestants don't call her Our Lady, and some of them don't like to talk about her at all. Are you Roman Catholic, too?" I shook my head. "I was brought up by an aunt--my mother is dead, too. Aunt Maddie talks a lot about religion, but I don't think she's a very good example of it. She's one of the people who doesn't like to talk about Mary. I'd like to know more about your religion and your life before and after you came to Oxford. I hope we'll be friends."

And we were. Dorothy was a rather brash and, in some ways, tactless young woman, but she had a good heart and I grew increasingly fond of her. My feelings about Somerville were a little more complex. Aunt Margot was so delighted with her visit because she envisioned an academic career for me. "You know Oxford still doesn't give women degrees, dear," she said, "but I hope that will change. And you can hear many of the same lectures and the exams are the same as for men. If you get First Class Honors in an examination you don't get an Oxford degree, but you've proved you're as intelligent as any man. And I think you're quite capable of getting a First, Vicky."

"I don't know, Margot" I said. "Aunt Maddie kept me at home. I've had no experience at school or examinations. I might take to it or I might not. In some ways I'd like a more outdoor life, and perhaps, in the long run, to write books like Jane Austin. Anyway, between the house and helping out Mr. Evans, I've got plenty to do right now. And perhaps some day I might write about things I'm doing now. Perhaps a novel set in ancient Crete, or a novel about good aunts and bad aunts." Margot laughed. "I hope I'm in the good aunt section." I gave her a hug. "At the top of the list so far as I'm concerned."

Actually, I was keeping myself busy. If all else failed, I could always read some of Uncle Petty's books. He had a very good scholarly library, but also had books on literature and history. I learned more about ancient Greek history from the books and found some delightful reading. I found George MacDonald's 'Curdie' books and renewed my acquaintance with Lewis Carroll's 'Alice' books which my mother had read to me when I was young. Uncle Petty also had some other books by Carroll: *Euclid and his Modern Rivals* which was a bit too much for me, *Sylvie and Bruno* which had some excellent parts but was no rival to the 'Alice' books and some writings about logic, which I found fascinating. Carroll's real name was Charles Dodgson and he had been a don at Christ Church.

When the long vacation came, Dorothy was going to spend it at home and she asked me if I would like to visit her there. "I can't spend the whole time with you," I told her. "I have to go to London to see my friend Robin and I don't like to leave Margot alone too long; but, yes, I'd like to see your home."

Kings Park was a mansion on the edge of Manchester, and I immediately liked Dorothy's father, Jeremiah King, who was a shrewd merchant who had made his fortune in trade and had retired to his mansion to enjoy it. The housekeeper was a widowed aunt of Dorothy's and I wasn't quite sure if she was a good aunt or a bad aunt. She was a kindly, hard working woman, but she had no patience with education for women and she never took Dorothy's education seriously. "Keeps her out of mischief until she gets a man," was all she could find to say about Dorothy's studies at Somerville.

Her father was less concerned about possible marriage. "Dorothy's a good girl," he told me one time when Dorothy was out of the room. "She's no need of a man to support her, and she wouldn't want to support a man. I'd like fine to keep her at home, it's the next best thing to having her mother here; but I don't want to stand in the way of anything she wants to do. I was thinking of taking her to Paris. You're about her age; if you were she would you like to go to Paris?" I smiled at him. "Mostly I've lived in London and Oxford and 'foreign parts' would interest me a lot. The place I'd really like to visit is Greece and Crete, which isn't officially a part of Greece yet, but perhaps soon will be. I've been doing some jobs for Mr. Evans, the Keeper of the Ashmolean Museum, and I've gotten really interested in Greece and Crete where he's been excavating.

He nodded. "Perhaps you're a bit more adventurous than Dot, but she might enjoy it if she had the right company..." I smiled at him and realized that if I didn't have my responsibility to Margot I could go to Crete. It would be interesting to see how it had changed. Of course, it would never do for a woman to travel alone. Dorothy would be a good companion on such a trip. Well, perhaps some day we could do it. "You never know," I said, "perhaps someday Dorothy and I will go to Crete." He nodded. "Aye, perhaps you will." he said.

I shared the thought with Dorothy and she was thrilled. "I don't know much about Crete," she said, "but I do know something about Greece. Wouldn't it be wonderful to see the Acropolis, not just pictures of it?" I remembered Alceme talking about 'the hill' in Athens and the high city on it. I now had learned enough Greek from Margot to realize that the word 'Acropolis' simply meant high city. I nodded. "Yes, it would," I said, "and I'd like to visit Mr. Evans excavations on Crete. Perhaps someday..." I'd have to investigate the costs of making the trip; I thought that Jeremiah King could afford to pay for Dorothy if I couldn't.

One of the interesting things about staying at King's Park was that Jeremiah had a lot of guests. Some were business people; what my Aunt Maddie would call people in trade. But a lot of them were artists or writers and Jeremiah would often sit such men at the table between Dorothy and I as a quiet way to help his daughter's education. One of the most interesting of these was a writer named Gilbert Chesterton. He was a friendly stout man with a walrus mustache and glasses hanging from a chain attached to his coat. Since he periodically took those off, and didn't seem able to find them until he remembered that they were attached to his coat, I suspected that someone, possibly his wife, had come up with the device to prevent him from losing them. He talked to Dorothy for a while and then turned to me. "I take it you aren't another King," he said. "No sign or red hair in Jeremiah or Dorothy." I laughed. "No, I'm a friend of Dorothy's staying here for a visit." He chuckled. "Nice family, the Kings," he said, "Miss Dorothy is a clever girl and old Jeremiah is the salt of the earth. A member of the jolly old upper middle class, as I am."

I smiled at him. "You're a writer, I've been told. Should I know any of your books?" He chuckled. "No obligation," he said, "I've probably spoiled more ideas for a good book than anyone I know. I've written some essays collected in books and studies of Watts and Browning. I'm a failed painter, went to the Slade Art School, and a not too successful poet. Nothing like failing at a subject to make you a good critic of the masters. And I've written a book called *The Napoleon of Notting Hill* which was the most fun I've had as a writer."

I privately decided to get some of his books; he seemed like an interesting man. "I've thought about doing some writing myself," I said. He smiled at me. "Get a job as a publishers reader: it will teach you how awful most writing is. But aside from that, just write. There's an old joke about how to become a writer: sit down and write for ten years. When you finally get up, you may be a writer." I thought of the things I'd written as a child, and even some things I'd written at Aunt Maddie's. "Well, I've been doing some private writing," I said. "That's the way," he said. "Did you publish a family magazine like Lewis Carroll?" I hesitated. "Once I did, before my parents died, but then I went to live with an aunt who didn't approve of young girls writing." He smiled. "You seem to have survived with your interest in writing undimmed. Will you write about votes for women, as Miss Dorothy wants to?"

I hesitated. "I'm not sure that I could add anything to what's been said by Mrs. Wollestonecroft and others. What do you think about votes for women?" He grinned at me. "To be in favor of votes for everyone is to be a supporter of democracy, but most women don't want the vote; so to be a true democrat, you have to give them what they want." This was an argument I hadn't even considered. Probably most women I knew were against votes for women, or indifferent to the whole issue. Didn't this man have a pretty good point?

Chapter Eleven

I rallied, "Don't you think women are worthy of the vote?" He gave me a serious look. "I think women are more than worthy of the vote. Women are the foundation of civilization, but I don't think the vote is worthy of them. Men have grown used to women pouring scorn on men's hobbies of sport and drinking and party politics. Now all of a sudden, along comes Miss Pankhurst who tells us that women were wrong, that party politics is to be taken seriously." I had some counter arguments against that, but I was distracted by his mention of Miss Pankhurst. "Do you know Christobel Pankhurst," I asked.

"Oh, yes," he said. He reached into his rather overstuffed pocket and came out with a piece of paper and a pencil, the kind artists use. On the back of the paper he drew a brilliant charicature of Christobel, with wild eyes and wild hair about her face, carrying a placard marked 'Votes for Women'." I burst out laughing. "I'd say that you're far from a failed artist," I told him. "May I keep this?" He presented it to me with a courtly bow which went rather oddly with his rather untidy appearance. "I'm sometimes asked to debate Miss Pankhurst or her mother or sister," he said. I think they tolerate me because I take their arguments seriously and pay attention to what they say."

"That's really the important thing to me," I said, "being taken seriously, not just dismissed because women aren't as strong as men." He gave a deep laugh. "If a man should vote because he's stronger, his horse ought to get two votes and his elephant, eight," he said.

I laughed in return. "But I know so few people who have their own elephant." He grinned at me. "I've often thought that pigs would be good pets," he said, but elephants would be even better. You could ride them to the grocer's and put all that you bought on their backs."

We had a very lively conversation after that: whatever his views on votes for women, he had a lively sense of humor, a keen mind and a great sense of the absurd side of things. After dinner the ladies withdrew to the sitting room while the men discussed sport and politics over their port and I felt some force to his earlier argument. This whole business of discussing sport and politics over drinks did strike me as absurd. Did I want to be invited to stay with the men to discuss boxing and racing and shooting? "It was good fun talking to you," I said. "I'd like to discuss some of this with you again. Did you give your argument to Dorothy?" He shook his head. "Oh, no. She's a true believer," he said. "I'd only disturb her simple faith in the Pankhurstian religion. But you have a good critical mind, and like me, you like to argue." My face reddened a little, but I was rather pleased by his words.

I didn't get another chance to talk to him then, and soon it was time for me to end my visit and go to London. Jeremiah waylaid me in the corridor and asked if he could speak to me in his 'bookroom' as he called his study. "Dot tells me that you want to see a friend in London," he said, "but that you may not have any place to stay." I said hesitatingly "Well, yes. My friend's house is closed because she and her mother are living at my aunt's, and even if there were room for me, I wouldn't like to live under my aunt's roof again." He nodded. "I'm thinking of taking Dot to London, seeing some shows and so on. I like your friendship with Dot: I'd like to encourage it. She hasn't had many friends who share her interests. I'll stay in a suite at Brown's Hotel, as I always do when I go the London, and there will be rooms for you and Dot. I'd appreciate it if you'd come to London and stay with us at Brown's."

It was a generous offer, and I was tempted. "I can pay for my own room," I said, "but I'd enjoy staying with you and Dorothy." He smiled at me. "Nay, Lass, I've plenty of brass," he said, "let me be your host." I could see that I might insult him by insisting, so I gave in with good grace; but I resolved to look around for a gift for him and Dorothy in return for his hospitality.

We went to London in a private railway carriage, and Brown's was an extremely elegant hotel. Jeremiah did indeed have 'plenty of brass' as he called money. When Robin and Dorothy met, I was a little apprehensive, but they got along well together after a few preliminary skirmishes and we soon became a threesome, with Jeremiah's benevolent eye on us. We had some very satisfactory shopping expeditions, and Jeremiah took us to some of the popular plays. Then one day Robin told Jeremiah, "There's a special performance of a play which Mrs. Langtry is taking to America. I know someone in the company, and I can get what they call 'house seats'. I'd like to take all five of us."

Jeremiah looked a little uncertain. "I'm not sure that one of Lilie Langtry's plays is quite the thing for the three of you," he said. "The king will be there,"

Robin said. Jeremiah laughed. "I'm not sure that's a recommendation," he said. "Ah, well, you're grown up girls and a play won't hurt you. Thank you, Miss Roberta."

Of course, Jeremiah took us all out to dinner with a carriage to take us to the theatre. "Rather a different meal than we had yesterday," Dorothy said demurely. At her father's inquiring look, she said, "We had fish and chips from a shop in the East End, rolled up in a newspaper. We ate it on the street." Jeremiah gave us a concerned look. "Aye, the fish and chips would be good. I've had many a meal like that, but I'm not sure I like you eating on the street in the East End." Dorothy told him, "Oh, we dressed very plainly and Vicky and Robin were doing their cockney accents. They're awfully good at it."

Jeremiah shook his head. "You three are a caution," he said. "Well, I suppose Miss Vicky and Miss Robin are experienced Londoners. I give it up." I knew what was bothering him. "Robin and I are very good at discouraging unwanted attentions, Mr. King, and with the three of us together, it's even easier. And there's my fictional brother, the all out bare knuckle boxer, who usually works very well." He shook his head. "It would be a brave man to get around the three of you," he said. "I won't worry any more, or at least not any more than any father would." I smiled at him. "We'll take good care of Dorothy," I told him. "Robin and I have been doing this for a long time. It's true that three 'ladies' in the East End might have some trouble, but three lively cockney girls with quick tongues are as safe as obvious 'ladies' would be in the West End--maybe safer. Robin and I started doing this because working class women have a lot more freedom of movement than a 'lady'."

Jeremiah nodded slowly. "Aye, I started off in the working class and have worked my way up to what my friend G.K.C. would call 'the jolly old upper middle class'. Perhaps it's good for Dot to see how the working class lives. Anyway, I might lose my brass and we'd have to go back to being working class. Plenty of people have. There used to be a saying 'From clogs to clogs in three generations' and it doesn't always take that long." I laughed. "You're a very generous man to your friends, but I'd back you against any enemies who tried to take away your money." He said with an expressionless face "I might just throw it away on taking young ladies out to dinner and such," but I knew when my leg was being pulled.

At the end of the play he reverted to the subject. "That Lillie Langtry is a stunner, isn't she? I can see a rich man becoming poor trying to satisfy her." he said. "Would you like to meet her?" asked Robin. "We've got an invitation backstage." Jeremiah looked at her for a moment. "I can't resist that," he said, "but you three will have to protect me."

We were admitted backstage through an inconspicuous door in the theatre. Robin was met with friendly grins: evidently she was a favorite with the porter and the stagehands. She knocked on a door and was told to come in. Lillie Langtry was there in an elaborate dressing gown, and the maid smiled at us from the background. "Lillie, here's Vicky and our new friend, Dorothy King, and her father, Jeremiah King."

Jeremiah bowed to Lillie with a dignified air. "In some theatres there'd be a star on that door, Mrs. Langtry," he said. Lillie laughed. "Oh, there will be in America," she said, "but this is just a farewell performance in a theatre that's not home to me any more." I hadn't seen Lillie with a man before, and you could almost feel the charm flowing out of her. It occurred to me that perhaps it was; that her charm might be a natural gift like being a beast wizard. "Didn't you run some race horses up in Manchester?" she asked Jeremiah. He nodded with an inexpressive face. "Aye, but it struck me that that's a good way for a rich man to lose his money."

Lillie laughed, then there was a light knock on the door and a man came in. Surely it wasn't---surely it couldn't be---but Lillie gave a little curtsey and said "I'd like you to meet my friends, Your Majesty, Jeremiah King and his daughter, Dorothy, and Miss Victoria Marsden and Miss Roberta Armitrage. Jeremiah bowed and Dorothy gave a formal curtsey, which Robin imitated in a rather flambouyant fashion. I bowed as Jeremiah had: Aunt Maddie had never taught us to curtsey. She probably thought that she and her family ought to be curtseyed to and we had never met Royalty (or ever expected to meet Royalty). The King bowed to us and shook Jeremiah's hand. "Quite a stunning trio, your daughter and her friends," he said. "You must have nipped through quite briskly: usually I get to Mrs. Langtry first." He turned to Lillie. "All the best on your trip to America, Lillie, and I hope that this performance helped."

She smiled at him. "Of course it has, sir. Americans 'love a lord' and the performance here with your majesties in attendance will make sure that our play will be a success in America." The King nodded. "Alexis and I were happy to do it." He turned to Jeremiah. "I know your name from somewhere." Jeremiah said, "Your Majesty addressed our committee on social reforms the last time you were in Manchester" The King nodded. "Shall I see your name on the honor's list," he asked. Jeremiah shook his head. "When your name is King an extra handle doesn't seem necessary. Besides, I'm not a heavy contributor to political parties."

The King looked at him. "I know that a lot of the names sent to me for the Honor's List are political, but we consider the names and we do try to honor those who deserve it even if there are no political motives." Jeremiah looked somewhat skeptical but did not reply. All of a sudden Dorothy burst out, "Your Majesty, what do you think of votes for women?" Immediately she reddened and looked terrified. The King gave her a keen glance but he was not one to crush butterflies any more than Gilbert Chesterton. "I don't think you need them," he said. "A woman has many ways of influencing those in power For example, if Lillie here brought something to my attention I'd take it very seriously." Dorothy blurted out, "But what about poor women, or women who aren't as beautiful as Mrs. Langtry?" The King smiled indulgently. "Very few women are that; but good men like your father here are trying to do things for poorer men and women." He turned to Lillie, "You know, you ought to introduce these three to some of your artist friends. Those pictures of you were the start of your career." Lillie looked at him and said "Berty" in a rather offended voice.

The King grinned, "I don't mean that they should retrace your career, my dear, though they could do worse. But three such pretty faces ought to be preserved." Jeremiah coughed. "You'll turn their heads, sir," he said. "Now the three of you and I had better clear off and let His Majesty congratulate Mrs. Langtry properly."

When we got outside the dressing room he said, half to himself, "I don't blame him, or her for that matter. What a pair of charmers." "Yes, aren't they," I replied. "You could almost feel their charm in the air." He nodded. "Well, he's a good King. His mother, your namesake would never let him have any office worthy of him before she died, and as a result he got up to a certain amount of mischief." He turned to Robin, "If I were your father, I'd want to know how you got to know Mrs. Langtrey." Robin grinned. "It was all due to our cockney act. I met Mrs. Langtry's maid at the bank." She went on to tell him the story and he laughed. "Well, I don't take it amiss that Dot is learning a bit more about life, but if any of you want to boast of our meeting the King to any of your female relatives, I'd alter the circumstances a bit."

"I know," I said. "Robin and I could never tell people like my aunts about our cockney adventures. We'll save any discussion of the King for people we love and trust." Jeremiah shook his head. "I'm not sure that you're not the center of this rather... unconventional... attitude, Miss Vicky. Most men wouldn't like it, you know." I chuckled, "That's why Dorothy and I want votes for women and some respect for women. Robin isn't quite sure yet, but we'll convert her." As a matter of fact, if any of us were going to retrace Lillie's career, I thought it might be Robin. Jeremiah laughed. "Well, a man who wouldn't respect you isn't for any of the three of you. Come away home."

Eventually I had to return and see how Margot was getting along. I left Robin in the hands of Jeremiah and Dorothy. Margot was delighted with my stories of life with them in London. "I know it's dreadful of me," she said, "but if I lived in classical times I think it would have been more interesting to be a 'companion' like Aspasia than a proper Athenian wife." I laughed. "Not all Athenian wives were quite that proper," I said, thinking of Alceme. "And it really does look from Mr. Evans' researches that women had a lot more respect in ancient Crete than they do now". I knew that from personal experience: any woman, but especially a priestess or a Leaper was treated with great respect in ancient Crete. I thought of the way such ladies were greeted in ancient Crete: a hand carried up to the forehead as if to shield the eyes, and the words "Bright Lady" murmured.

It was almost time for Lillie to leave for America and I was thinking about whether I could get away to see her off. One day, working at the Ashmolean, a museum guard came to me and said, "You're wanted on the instrument." That meant the telephone, and I wondered who could be calling me. Lillie's familiar voice came over the line. "Vicky, Robin's mother has suddenly died. Could you come to London. She really needs you."

Chapter Twelve

When I got to London, I went straight to Brown's Hotel where Robin was being cared for by Dorothy. "I'm some help," she said, "but you're a much older friend. Partly, she blames herself for moving her mother to your aunt's. I don't know why." When I did talk to Robin, her reasons were rather confused. "We kept her off the drink," she said, "but your Aunt Ceal pampered her: gave her chocolates and other sweetmeats. She ate better than she ever has, of course, but you know the strain of living with your Aunt Maddie. Mother was getting fat, but she seemed rather listless. Any little effort would make her stop and take deep breaths. Did moving her to your aunt's house hasten her end? I don't know if I could ever go back to that house."

"I have an idea about that," I said. "You get some rest now and we'll talk tomorrow." Brown's, of course, was on the telephone, and I called Lillie from the cubicle in the lobby. "Lillie, would you take Robin to America with you?" I asked. "Like a shot," Lillie said. "Do you think we can persuade her?" In the end, we did. A week or so at sea and the new experiences in America would distract her. I hated parting with her, and Lillie too, but Lillie had to work to keep up that beautiful house, and I thought that Robin was half blaming me for her mother's death. I had done the negotiating that led to her mother's stay in the house and she seemed to blame that for her mother's death. Better to be separated for a while and get back together when her mind was clearer; I didn't want to quarrel with her.

Lillie told me just before she left, "I'll talk to her on the boat and in America. I'll say her mother died because of a heart seizure. Getting fat didn't help, but the rackety life she led before was mostly to blame. Robin shouldn't blame herself or you. I think you're too sensible to blame yourself."

"I acted for what I thought was the best," I said. "I'm not much for self blame." Lillie laughed, "Nor am I. In one of my houses there was a motto painted on the wall 'So they say...let them say'. Bertie built that house for me. You can see how I was attracted to him, now you've met him." I nodded, "Indeed I do; he's a fine man still, and as a young man he must have been almost irresistible. Lillie, forgive my impertinence, but do you and he still..." She laughed. "Once in a while," she said, "but it's more for old times sake now. The important thing is that he's a good friend, and always will be. You know, Vicky, that was one of the reasons for liking you so much. You've been a good friend to Robin and your Aunt Margot. Tell me, do you have a lot of men who are fond of you and ask you to call them 'uncle'." I thought of Uncle Vester and Uncle Arthur. "Well, yes," I said, "but they don't..." She smiled, "Of course not. Your apparent innocence is part of your charm, rather like Alice in the Lewis Caroll books. When you meet a man who can see you as you really are and still love you, you'll know you've got the right man."

I wasn't quite prepared to discuss men with Lillie, though I remembered Helen saying that Odysseus had seen her as she was and still respected her. "I'm not aware that I have any charm," I said. Lillie laughed.

"That's part of your charm," she said. "I'll take good care of Robin and you take good care of Dorothy. I wish you could come with us, but you have your obligations to your Aunt Margot. Maybe on another tour." I smiled, "I'll live in hope. You're a good friend to all three of us, Lillie, and I'll be longing to see you again." Lillie hugged me and I went off feeling much better about Robin. Lillie Langtry knew a lot about hearts, and I thought she could help Robin to recover, possibly better than I could in the circumstances.

Dorothy and I explored London as Robin and I had, and it was great fun. But one day he fun stopped. Dorothy and I were traveling on the two-penny tube, which was always a bit of an adventure, and when we got off, I came face to face with the loutish man who had been with Mumford when I turned their own dogs on them. "Well, well," he said, "the little beast wizard. If you can do that to dogs, perhaps you can do it with horses, too. Come along with me, deary, and your friend, too. I want to try some experiments."

I looked around. At this time of day there were very few travelers on the tube, most of them women. There was a woman carrying a black and white cat in a basket, and I reached out for its mind. The cat jumped out of the basket onto the loutish man's head and began clawing and spitting. He was completely taken aback: he began clawing at his head, shouting words which I hoped Dorothy didn't know. "Come on Dorothy, *run*," I said. We ran for the exit to the tube station, but in a minute I heard boots thumping on the ground behind us. We must have taken a wrong turn, because I could see a blank wall ahead of us.

The Gryphon Seal

"Chryseis, can you help?" I thought frantically. With renewed hope, I saw the shadowy tunnel open up before me, and grasping Dorothy's hand I ran down it. The sound of pursuing footsteps faded, and as we went on I could see sunlight at the end of the tunnel. We ran toward it and came out on a beach. Near us was a horse-drawn chariot with two familiar figures in it, Helen, looking not a day older than she had when I knew her on Crete, and still as beautiful as ever, and M'pha, not so much looking older, as a great deal more mature. Both were looking at us with no appearance of surprise. The shadowy tunnel had vanished, and a long, lovely beach stretched as far as the eye could see.

"See, I told you that Chryseis would do it," Helen said to M'pha. "I think she left the path that Vicky came through somehow connected to the ring. At a time of great need, it would open for her." M'pha leaped from the chariot and we hugged. She turned to Dorothy. "Has Vicky told you about her previous visits to our time?" she asked, taking Dorothy's hand in her own.

"She's told me a lot about ancient Crete," Dorothy faltered, "but I thought they were just stories. Now I see they weren't." She stared at Helen. "Who is that beautiful woman?" she asked. "Helen of Sparta" said M'pha, "and Helen of Troy, though she doesn't like that name." Dorothy moved toward Helen as if hypnotized, and M'pha gave a quiet chuckle. "She's Helen-struck," she said. "Something like being nymph-struck, but less fatal. It's men usually, but some women fall victim, also. The man I was going to marry was Helen-struck at first, but he finally noticed me." I looked at her. "The man you *were* to marry?" I asked. She nodded and said, "I'll tell you all about it, Vicky. In fact, I'm so glad you're here. Helen has her problems with men, but not quite this problem."

"Helen of Troy," I said. "Then the war has already happened?" She nodded. "Yes, I was with Helen in Troy. My mother made me promise to stay with her until she was rescued by Menelaus. We've grown very close, but as I say, she doesn't quite have my problems. You look about the same, Vicky. It hasn't been long in your time since you visited us last?" I shook my head. "No, less than a year; but I've met the king of my country, and a woman who is almost as beautiful as Helen, and I've had some problems with men. Isn't it wonderful to be able to talk." She grasped my arm. "It is indeed," she said. "Don't worry about your friend; Helen is very kind to those who are Helen-struck. Your friend will hardly notice if we two go off. Let's walk along the beach."

We set off down the beach, and M'pha said, "Let me give you an idea of my biggest problem. I was engaged to Telemachus, Odysseus' son, but he was disappointed in me and I in him. I wonder if I didn't agree to marry him because of Odysseus, who is quite a remarkable man, and his wife, Penelope, is a dear. I would have liked being their daughter-in-law. Perhaps I wanted that more than I wanted Telemachus, which is not such a good reason for marriage. When Telemachus and I started to quarrel, I made the absolutely fatal mistake of comparing him to his father. It's something he's very sensitive about, and I should never have let those

The Gryphon Seal

words cross my lips...." She trailed off and I thought it best to change the subject for a while.

"Tell me about Odysseus," I said. "He and Helen are still remembered in my time." Her face lit up. "He and Helen are really responsible for the fall of Troy. He said, when Helen agreed to help him, that the war at Troy was almost over. And it was. Is the Trojan Horse still remembered in your day?" I nodded, "Indeed it is, though lots of people thought it was a myth. But there's a learned man in our time who has excavated the ruins of Troy and another, a friend of mine, who excavated the ruins of Knossos.

M'pha gave a little shudder. "Talking about the ruins of Troy and especially Knossos gives me a sinking feeling. What kind of people live in Crete in your time?" I said, "The descendants of your Cretans, I think, along with some Hellenes who invaded Crete later. Crete is independent now, but it may join the Hellenic state that covers most of what you would think of as Hellenic lands. The Cretans just won a battle against some invaders who ruled Crete for a long time and have won their freedom." M'pha looked more cheerful. "If the people of Crete still love and fight for freedom, they aren't so different from the present Cretans. It makes sense that all the Hellenic lands are united in one state. Not long ago Theseus took all of Attica under Athenian leadership." I nodded. "Athens is the capital of the Hellenic Kingdom now. Their present ruler is a relative of our king." M'pha smiled. "That sounds more cheerful. You know, Mother was Athenian and father came from Crete, and before Decalion became Minos there was a sort of union between Athens and Crete under Theseus. It doesn't sound as if the Hellenes have changed much either."

"If I get back to my own time, I plan to visit Crete and the Hellenic Kingdom." I said. M'pha looked at my finger. "Vicky, you've got your ring back. I left it in safe keeping in Knossos before I started my travels to Sparta and Troy." I chuckled. "Very safe keeping, M'pha" I said. "It was dug up a second time from the ruins of Knossos by my Uncle Arthur." She shook her head. "I don't want to think about that ring and its travels in time. There must be two of them now: the one you have on and the one I left in Knossos. It makes my head ache to think about it." I laughed. "It makes my head ache to think of my travels in time," I said, "but I'm very glad to be here and see you again."

She nodded. "I really needed you," she said, "and I wouldn't be surprised if Chryseis didn't bring you back to this time because I needed you." I shook my head. "How does Chryseis do these things," I asked. "Her parents were mortal, weren't they?" She hesitated, then said, "Not quite. Her mother was an Olympian who gave up her immortality to live with her father who was mortal. That's one reason I quarreled with Telemachus. It's hard to explain, but you have had experience of a Path, the one that brought you to this time and back again. Well, Paths don't always cross from one time to another. Some of them lead from this world to others: the Bright Land where the Olympians live and the Dark Land where the rebellious Titans are imprisoned. When Chryseis came to Crete, she was able to walk the Path to the Bright Land and live in it. That's what makes her an Olympian--even a little of the direct light of the Bright Land is fatal to most mortals. My brother has a scar where a tiny chink of light from there fell on his skin; I'll tell you about it presently."

"So this Bright Land is where people like Chryseis disappear to when they vanish from our world," I asked, "and it gives them their powers?" She nodded. "More or less," she said. "I'll tell you more later. Well, after Telemachus and I were engaged, we visited my relatives on Crete. There's a very important Path leading from the Room of the Path in Knossos. I've heard stories about it all my life from Chryseis and Ariadne. So Telemachus and I decided to go down the path together, if it would open for us. It did and we started off for the Bright Land."

"And if you discovered that you could live in the Bright Land, you could do all the things Chryseis does--you'd be a goddess." I said. "It's a little more complicated than that," she said. "You have to have permission from the Council of Olympus to live there. Chryseis took her mother's place as an Olympian so that the Council could permit her mother to give up immortality and live with Chryseis' father. But, yes, if you can live in the Bright Land, you can be an Olympian. After walking down the Path for a while, Telemachus and I were stopped by a male Olympian--I think it might have been Hermes. He told us that only one of us could live in the Bright Land, the other would die there, but he didn't say which of us could live there."

"Oh, M'pha," I said, "what a terrible choice to have to make, to be a god or goddess or to stay with the one you love, unless you were really head over heels in love with the other person to make it an easy choice." She sighed, "Well, I had been brought up on Chryseis' stories and I waited for Telemachus to say that he'd give up immortality for me...and he didn't. We quarreled there on the path. That's when I told him he wasn't the man his father was. I went back to our world and found myself on Naxos, where Ariadne and Dion were having one of their Dances, but even that didn't help. I came back then, here to Sparta, because Helen is my best friend in this time. I longed to talk to you, and now you're here."

Making mental notes to ask for further explanation of half a dozen points in her story, I tried to give her what advice I could. "I recall some stories you told me on my last trip. When Chryseis' mother, Aphea, gave up her immortality, hadn't she known Chryseis' father, Lykos, for a while, and wasn't Chryseis already born? You told me that Aphea and Lykos were part of the triumvirate who rule Caria. So if that's true, they met, fell in love, and lived together for eight years before Aphea had to go back. Don't you think that you were holding up Telemachus to rather high standards to expect him to give up the hope of immortality for himself immediately on hearing that news?" I asked.

"Perhaps you're right, Vicky" she replied. "Perhaps we'd have had to know each other better to make it an easy choice. I suppose I expected him to say he'd rather be with me than be an Olympian, and I could protest and..." I stopped her. "You're assuming that you couldn't live in the Bright Land. Why?"

She looked surprised. "Well, there was my brother Ducalion and what happened to him, and even though his wife Acame could perhaps live in the Bright Land--she's Ariadne's niece--I don't think she even thought of it." I interrupted her, " So you had the romantic idea that he could be an Olympian and you expected him to immediately react by giving it up for you. Could it be that he, for some reason, thought it was you who could live in the Bright Land, and didn't want to influence you to give it up?"

M'pha hugged me and said, "I never even thought of that, You're so sensible, Vicky. Now I know why Chryseis brought you to me. Of course it was unfair of me to judge Telemachus like that and I at least owe him the chance to discuss it with me. Maybe I've been completely unfair to him. At least we ought to talk about it. Vicky, Telemachus is in Athens. Will you come to Athens with me and help us to discuss it calmly?"

Chapter Thirteen

"Of course I will," I said, "but won't Helen miss you?" She shook her head. "Helen was looking forward to my living with Telmachus and being happy with him. Anyway, I haven't exactly been a little ray of sunshine since I returned. Helen and I will always be friends: we've been through so much together. She and Menelaus are so happy together and she'd like to see me happy, too. She'll gladly let me go. Bring your friend from your own time if you like, but I think at her present stage of being Helen-struck she won't want to leave Helen." I asked her, "Helen and Menelaus are happy together?" She nodded, "Very happy." I hesitated. "When we first met Helen she seemed a little ambiguous about him her feelings for him," I said.

M'pha laughed, and it was good to hear her laugh. That feeling I had that she had matured was partly due to her having suffered, I realized. Her expression, instead of being bright and eager, was serious and rather sad. "You remember, she said if a man says he is in love with you, you're never sure if it's you or your beauty he loves? Well, toward the end of the war she lost her beauty ,or appeared to have lost it. It turned out that Menelaus did love her. Helen or I will tell you about it."

When we asked Helen if we could go to Athens, she said, "Of course. I'll have Menelaus give you one of his best ships, and we'll send some guards and attendants with you so the Athenians will give you proper respect. I think perhaps Menelaus and I will visit Athens soon, but when you're a reigning monarch you can't go off on impulse; things have to be prepared for a state visit. Vicky, will you leave Dorothy with me for a while? I'd like to get to know her." With a certain amount of relief, I said, "Of course," and didn't miss the look of relief on Dorothy's face; she wouldn't have to be parted from her current idol.

In the stir of getting ready for our return to the palace, I was left alone with Helen for a few moments. "Bless you, Vicky," she said to me. "M'pha looks happier than she has since she came back from Naxos. I have a feeling I might be needed in Athens: Telmachus has sent me a curious letter. I'll take good care of Dorothy. Even though we have to part so soon, I'm glad you came back to our time." I told her, "So am I, Helen. You look wonderful, as usual. It's hard to believe that you lost your beauty for a while." She chuckled. "It was a highly illuminating experience, but the best thing was that Menelaus still loved me, and chose me over what seemed to be me with my beauty intact. Yes, I don't change. Perhaps I can persuade Menelaus that we can live in the Bright Land some day."

"And if you can't?" I asked. She smiled at me. "Then I'll stay with him, of course. So M'pha has already told you about the problem between Telemachus and her. It took me weeks to pry it out of her. You're good for each other, Vicky." I laughed. "M'pha has certainly been good for me. At Chryseis' suggestion, she helped me develop my tauromathic power which has saved me from some awkward situations of late. I've met a woman almost as beautiful as you, but she's getting older and isn't quite as beautiful as she was as a girl; I've seen pictures of her." Helen nodded. "That's how I consoled myself when I lost my beauty; most women lose theirs with aging."

When we got back to the palace, Helen told M'pha to find suitable quarters for us and to show them to Dorothy. "I have something I want to show Vicky," she said. We went to her rooms, which were as beautifully decorated as Lillie's, but with less clutter. She took me to her dressing table and picked up a mirror; a kind I had seen in Crete, with one silver side and one golden side. She gazed steadily into the silver side, then turned around and faced me.

Her beauty was gone; she looked like a friendly intelligent person, but the unmatched perfection of her face was gone. "If Menelaus decides not to go the Bright Land I'll have to use this. It was given to me by someone I regarded as an enemy at the time, but I'm not so sure now that she wasn't a friend." I looked at her. "Your voice is still beautiful, and the way you carry yourself." She laughed. "Menelaus told me that he felt the same when I lost my beauty, bless him. If you ever find a man who'll love you even if the reason for his loving you seems to have disappeared, latch on to him, Vicky. Such men are very rare, and I hope Telmachus is one of them." She looked steadily into the golden side of the mirror and her beauty came back.

"Does that only work for you?" I asked. She chuckled. "Fortunately or unfortunately, only for me. M'pha tried it once. She looked the same, no matter how much she looked into either side. On the whole, I was relieved. Think of what a prize a mirror which could make an ugly woman beautiful or a beautiful woman ugly would be. I'm not sure that wars wouldn't be fought over it.

"I don't think you should should show this to Dorothy, "I said. "M'pha and I value you for other qualities you have, but Dorothy sees only your beauty." Helen grinned. "Thank you, my dear. It's nice to be valued for something else besides my beauty. One of the reasons I like Odysseus is that he tells me he values my wisdom and compassion over my beauty. I didn't always like him: when he was one of my official courtiers before I married Menelaus I was rather offended when he chose my cousin Penelope over me. And he made a remark that got back to me that a woman as beautiful as me didn't need to think about things."

I hesitated. "Dorothy is involved in a struggle in our own time to get some respect for women. If she talks to you about it, try to help her. I'd be interested in what you have to say, too." She sighed. "It's a problem, even here in Sparta and almost everywhere in the Hellenic world, except for Crete which is becoming more Hellenic and less fair to women. I'll talk to her about it, but I'm not sure I can help. Men think they should rule because they're physically stronger."

"I was talking to a man who isn't completely on our side and he pooh-poohed that argument. He said that if men should be important because of strength, then their horses should be twice as important and their elephants, if they have any, should be even more important." She laughed. "He sounds like a witty, if not a wise man. About Dorothy: I'll let her get used to me before I raise any questions about beauty."

I only stayed in Sparta a short time before M'pha and I were off on a ship to Athens, but I could see what Helen meant. Men ate together, laughed together, and probably regarded women only for their beauty and their useful qualities. I mentioned this to M'pha. "Yes," she said, "it's one of the things that makes staying here with Helen a bit of a burden. It's hard to have a man as a friend here, though you and I know we had many male friends when we were Leapers in Crete." I asked, somewhat tentatively, "Did you ever make love to a man, M'pha?" She shook her head. "When we were Leapers I was the tauromath and it's a well known story that female and even male tauromaths lose their power if they lose their virginity. Then, when I spent ten years in Troy with Helen, I was regarded as a sort of servant because I was her handmaid. Not much chance to form a lasting relationship there, anyway. Then I came to visit Helen here and met Telemachus and he seemed different. I'm a dozen years older than he is, but Helen, along with some of her Olympian friends, was able to give me some help in staying young.

"But you could talk with Telemachus, and laugh with him?" I asked. She nodded. "Yes, I could. Perhaps I've done him an injustice with my romantic notion that he should have immediately declared that he didn't want immortality if I couldn't have it. But the wisest thing you've said, Vicky, is that he may have assumed for some reason that I could be immortal and he couldn't. If that's what he thought, I've really been unjust to him."

Spartans are not great seamen, so the ship that M'pha and I took to Athens was sailed by Cretans in the service of Menelaus and Helen. Everyone on board was highly respectful to M'pha as a former Leaper, and to me when she introduced me as one of her Leapers. My youthful appearance may have raised some questions, but those in the service of Sparta were used to the unchanging beauty of Helen, and M'pha also never seeming to age. When we got to Athens, we were regarded as ambassadors from Sparta preparing for a state visit by Helen and Menelaus, so were treated respectfully. We had many offers to show us the city, but M'pha laughed. "My mother was Alceme, daughter of Academus, the Councilor," she said. "I probably know Athens as well as any of you." That caused even greater respect; evidently Alceme was a semi-legendary heroine in Athens. Alceme was not one of my close friends as M'pha, Robin, and Dorothy were, but she along with Helen and Lillie were women I loved and respected. Ariadne and Chryseis, who were Olympians now, I felt were in a special category.

M'pha took me, along with some of our guards who were Cretan like the crew of our ship, up to the Acropolis. Men and women had lived there within living memory and the king's palace had been there. Now it was more and more a place dedicated to the gods, and the everyday life of the city was centered around the new royal palace and the marketplace, both near the foot of the hill.

I was used to pictures of the Parthenon in books, but although there was a temple to Athena here, it was smaller and less perfect than the Parthenon. There was a temple on the site of the Erechtheun, but it did not have the beauty of the Erectheum which had survived to my own time. I knew that the Parthenon and Erectheum, which I knew, had been built in the reign of Pericles, many centuries in the future from the time I was in. Some of the greatest sculptors and architects of Greece had worked on what were now ruins in my time

Still, there was a rather homey feeling to this older Acropolis; more like a parish church than a cathedral. We were on our way to the temple of Athena, when I heard a shout. "M'pha." A magnificent man, who looked about the age of King Edward, but had an even greater air of command, came up to M'pha and hugged her. "Oh, Odysseus," she said. I knew that this was one of M'pla's heroes, and I didn't want to intrude on their reunion. "I'll be inside the temple," I said, and turned away.

The inside of the temple was not really like a church, but more like a public building. Men and a few women strode up and down outside it, laughing and chattering; very much the atmosphere of the Great Court at Knossos. The inside of the temple was empty except for one figure. It was dominated by a large statue of Athena, not one I recognized. This statue must have been destroyed by the Persians when they looted and destroyed the Acropolis. Still, the statue looked somehow familiar. It was the face; a rounded chin and a keen look in the eyes, which seemed to follow you. Then I looked at the figure near the base of the statue and saw the same rounded chin and keen expression. It was Chryseus!

"I fill in for my Aunt Athena sometimes," she said. "I thought I'd link the Path to the ring and it would help you in a moment when you needed to avoid

The Gryphon Seal

danger. I had ways of knowing that you'd got the ring back. You brought a friend with you: she's in good hands with Helen." Wishing I knew how she knew all these things, I spoke. "Not only did the ring save me from pursuit when Dorothy and I came here, but your casual suggestion the M'pha that I get some training as a tauromath paid off, too."

She smiled. "Perhaps it wasn't so casual, Vicky. Even if one can't see the future, as Apollo does, one gets certain hunches. I'm afraid that this is your final visit to this age unless certain rather unlikely events happen. I'll get you and your friend to our time when you're ready to go. Both of you near the same time, but not quite the same place; probably an open space near where you left." I nodded. "Yes, one of our parks would do well. Will we just appear out of the air? Do our physical bodies make the journey in time?"

She nodded. "Yes, they do, but there are ways of seeing that the Path doesn't drop you where people can see you, or near any danger." I laughed. "Yes, Dorothy and I were running from pursuit when the Path opened up. I'd just as soon not have to go back into that situation. Thank you for everything, Chryseis. You said you'd bring me back so I could see M'pha again, and you did. I suppose I can't spend my life shuttling between here and my own time." She shook her head. "No, I don't have that feeling about you. I think you came to this time to learn certain things which you will be able to use in your own time. But I have something to show you". She extended her right hand, and on it was...my ring! I looked down at my own left hand and the ring was there, too!

"This was given to me by my friend Hephestus, the smith of the gods, as some people call him. It's a celebration of an anniversary, and it was made only a few days ago. At some time I'll leave it in Knossos, where it will be dug up by your friend. Then you'll come into possession of it, bring it back to our time, and give it to M'pha. She'll leave it in safe keeping in Knossos where it will be dug up a second time and come into your possession again."

I looked at the figure on the ring. "The girl riding the gryphon--is that you?" She smiled. "Yes, when I first got to the Bright Land I met a gryphon, did him a small service, and was rewarded with the help and friendship of the gryphons. I like to ride gryphons if they ask me, and I'm almost the only one who does. Even apart from the fact that Hephaestus made it for me, it's a pretty good bet that a girl riding a gryphon is meant for me. If you look very closely at the figure on the gryphon, you'll see that it has my face. Do you have ways of making something small appear large in your time?"

"Yes, I said, "and my friend, the man who dug it up, has weak eyes for everyday vision, but if he holds something near his eyes he can see it better than anyone can ordinarily." She nodded. "I can make my eyes do that," she said, "it's part of our Olympian powers. But more and more I think that things which can only be done by Olympians in this time, will more and more be done by mortals by natural means. How do you make things appear larger?" I looked at her. "We call them lenses--usually made of glass--you have glass in this time." She nodded. "Possibly not as good as in your time, but Egyptians especially can work in glass. They often make small containers out of glass-- perfume bottles and such. You may have seen them at Knossos."

"Of course," I said, "Ariadne had some and I believe M'pha has at least one. Even without a lens, you can see that the ring you have is new, while mine has suffered from scratches. In fact, there's a little scratch I made when I was leaping a bull on my first visit, which tells me that this is the second appearance of the ring." She nodded. "Good thinking. So although we have this ring going back and forth in time, we do know its origin: Hephestus made it for me. In fact, when you had it on your previous visits, it came back before it was made, but that's the nature of time travel into the past. You won't be born for many centuries but here you are. There's one other thing about the ring: if you go the Bright Land, it'll shelter you against the light of the True Sun. Even if you couldn't ordinarily live there, the ring will protect you. Odysseus has one like it which Circe gave him." "Odysseus is outside, talking to M'pha," I said. "Yes," she said, "I know he is, but I don't want to meet him."

Chapter Fourteen

I looked at her. "Is Odysseus an enemy of yours?" I asked. She shook her head. "Quite the reverse: he's the only man I've ever fallen in love with and would want to marry, but he has a wife, Penelope, and chose to go back to her. I'd love to talk to him, but, on the whole, I think it's better that we avoid meeting, at least for a while. Perhaps some day I'll find one of the other Olympians to marry, and then it may be safer to meet him." I looked at her compassionately. "I guess even being an Olympian doesn't protect you from falling in love with a married man."

She said slowly, "There are ways that some Olympians might take--killing Penelope by some apparently natural means and leaving Odysseus free. If he were free he'd marry me." I shook my head. "You wouldn't do that, Chryseis; you're too honest. Besides, think of how it would feel to get Odysseus that way." She smiled at me. "You have a lot of sense, Vicky," she said. "I don't know if I'm as honest as you think, but no, I wouldn't get Odysseus that way: it would poison our whole friendship and I know we'll always be friends even if we can't be lovers. You're a good person to talk to, Vicky, and you have your own kind of wisdom. Do you know why M'pha and Telemachus broke up?"

"Yes," I said, "they were on their way on a Path to see what they could of the Bright Land. M'pha knows the dangers; her brother discovered that he couldn't live in the Bright Land when one little ray of sunshine from there made a scar on his skin." I shuddered. "Think of the damage it would have done if he'd have stepped out into the sunlight. An Olympian met them and told them that only one of them could live in the Bright Land. They quarreled and parted. I've suggested to M'pha that perhaps Telemachus thought that it was she who could live in the Bright Land, but she had the romantic notion that they should have each declared that they wouldn't want immortality without the other, and in typically feminine fashion, she waited for him to go first."

Chryseis sighed. "She was brought up on stories of how my mother gave up her Olympian status to stay with my father, but they'd been in love for a while and I was already born when she made that decision. I think you're right , Vicky: it was a romantic notion to expect that to be his first reaction. If she'd spoken first---but as you say, most women want their lovers to offer a sacrifice, rather than to be shamed into it by example. I'd just as soon know the facts and make my decision on that basis, but then some people think I'm not feminine enough."

"I think M'pha should find out which one of them can live in the Bright Land and then talk to Telemachus," I said. "Would she have to go back to Knossos to do that?" Chryseis shook her head. "Oh, no, there's a Path from here; I can let her enter it, but I don't like letting her go alone and I don't think it's a good idea, for various reasons, for me to take her. Vicky, could you be her companion on the journey?"

"Of course," I said, "even apart from my love for M'pha, I'd love to see the Bright Land where you Olympians live." She shook her head. "There are a lot of dangers on the Path to the Bright Land. The Dark Powers will try to stop you, and even the Olympians may put obstacles in your way." I nodded. "Yes, I know it's not just a sightseeing visit, but I'd still like to see, and if M'pha needs me..."

"All right," she said, "I suspect that this is some kind of Olympic test for M'pha and Telemachus. It wasn't just an oversight when Hermes, if that's who it was, didn't tell them who could live in the Bight Land. You may have to meet some challenges from the Dark Powers or the Olympians to get there and back: but cheer up; they can only give you three tests each way." I smiled, somewhat wryly. "Only three each way. Well, at least it's limited number." She smiled and touched my arm. "That's why I want M'pha to have a companion. They know her weaknesses, but as a time traveler you're an unknown factor to them." I nodded. "Yes, so I can really help M'pha then. Of course I'll do it." She nodded. "No time like the present," she said. "M'pha will be here in a minute looking for you. Can you persuade her without me. I don't like to use my old relationship with her, or any supposed Olympian wisdom, to persuade her that she ought to go."

I nodded. Chryseis gave me a hug, then vanished, leaving a few golden motes floating in the air. Hardly had they faded, when M'pha came into the temple looking very distressed. "I couldn't tell Odysseus," she said, "and he didn't try to make me tell him why Telemachus and I separated. He only said that he and Penelope will still love me even if I don't marry Telemachus. In some ways that's what I want, to be in the place of a daughter to both of them; but what about

Telemachus?" I took her hands in mine. "M'pha, you've got to know the facts before you can make any decision. Why don't we try to get to the Bright Land through the Path here in the temple. We can do as your brother did; get close to the end of the Path and see if you can stand the light of the Bright Land."

Her face lilt up. "That's a marvelous idea, Vicky. If it's not me who can live in the Bright Land, I can tell Telemachus and see what his reaction is. If it is me, that makes a greater problem. Before we quarreled I'd have immediately renounced living in the Bright Land for him--now I'm not so sure. But it will be good to know. Menesthius, the friend of Theseus, and the uncle of the present ruler of Athens, always said it was better to know the facts, and it would be something that might make it easier to make up my mind. But there are dangers on the Path to the Bright Land." I nodded. "I've been told about them, but if you want to go, I'll go with you. I think my ring will be of some help on the Path."

She nodded. "Odysseus has a ring like yours. He said it enabled him to walk the Path and learn from his experiences there. He said he'd tell me all about it when we had time." "Is his ring just like mine?" I asked. "No, it has a gryphon on it but no rider, and it's more square and massive than yours." I laughed. "I'm just as glad," I said. "There are enough of this ring to give me a headache. How do we get on to the Path?" She said, "It's probably just behind the big statue of Athena. Luckily there are no officials here or we wouldn't be allowed back there." We climbed into the niche behind the statue, facing the wall of the treasury where gifts to Athens were kept. "I don't know if we can use it without some kind of ceremony," she said, but there before us was not the wall, but a shadowy tunnel which both of us recognized. "All right," I said, "here we go."

We walked down the shadowy tunnel. "If it forks, we have to always keep to the right. Going to the left would bring us to the Dark Land and from what Ducalion told me we definitely don't want to go there. From Ducalion and my mother, I know that there might be tests to face," M'pha said. "It would be too easy otherwise," I said. "We can't go the whole way without some risk." The first was when I saw a figure ahead of us blocking the Path. It was Aunt Maddie, with her most severe look on her face. She was pointing back to where we had come in. "M'pha," I said, "do you see a figure ahead of us?"

"Yes," she said, "it's my grandmother, looking very incensed and waving me back to the entrance." I gave a hollow laugh. "I see my Aunt Maddie," I said. "Your grandmother brought you up after Alceme left, didn't she?" M'pha was grim. "She tried," M'pha said, "but it was a constant battle." I nodded. "Each of us is seeing an authority figure from our past trying to get us to go back." M'pha grinned. "They don't seem to know that we've always been as rebellious as we are now. I think that we should just keep on walking. I think these figures are just illusions, and we can walk right through them." We did, and they vanished when we were a few feet away. "If that's the best they can do..." I said, but the corridor ahead of us seemed to be a small room with two figures in it. As we got closer,

The Gryphon Seal

I saw that the figures were Alceme and Artimodorus in some kind of consultation. I heard Alceme's voice, "I wouldn't make Vicky the next Leaper, Artimodorus. She's actually afraid of animals and all she can do is a side leap." Artimodorus shook his head. "She has a lot of spirit and I like her. She'll overcome that fear of animals and become a better Leaper with practice." The figure who looked like Alceme shrugged and said with that faint drawl in her voice, which was sometimes highly irritating, "You're the Master of the Dance, but I'd advise against it." The figures vanished, and M'pha turned to me in indignation. "If my mother actually said that, she was wrong. You're not afraid of animals, and you can do a very good head leap. I'm sorry, Vicky." "Don't worry about it," I said. "When they asked me to be a Leaper I *was* afraid of animals: my Aunt Maddie wouldn't even have a cat in the house, and I think at one time I was frightened by a black dog. Remember how formidable the bulls looked when you first saw them, and all I could do on my first visit here *was* a side Leap--I never got beyond that. When I traveled back and met with you, I had the experience of my first visit to build on, and I'd grown up a little. If your mother did say that, she was right, and when I did become a Leaper she was always helpful and friendly. I think they're trying to make us quarrel with each other."

She looked thoughtful. "Yes, I think they are. They didn't know that you'd be the one to defend my mother. Besides, this, if it happened, was taken out of context. I think some of the conversations we had about some of the others in our company would have made them angry if they'd been overheard." I smiled at her. "You're mother may have been playing devil's advocate, making Artimodorus defend his choice of me. Don't worry about it."

The next illusion shook me a little more. There were two figures in a bed, the man kissing the girl and stroking her breasts. He rolled on top of her: I felt like a voyeur, especially since the woman was M'pha. Had she lied to me about never having made love to a man? When the vision vanished, M'pha said, "It wasn't what it looked like, Vicky. That was Telemachus, and when things got to that stage, he got up from the bed and took me for a walk. He said he didn't want to force me into anything, and he could wait till we were married, but if he had insisted..." I touched her arm. "Don't worry, M'pha. What goes on between engaged couples is none of my business, and even if you had lied to me about never having made love to a man, that's easily forgiven. That was your business, not mine." I didn't say that I had observed that they both wore their Leaper's kilts, which are not all that easy to get off. Even if they had been naked, I would have accepted M'pla's word. "You know," she said, "that was one thing that made me love Telemachus, that he didn't take advantage of me when he might have. It wasn't just that we weren't married, mother conceived Ducalion before she and father married, but I really wasn't ready for it".

"You know, showing us those two scenes was really a foul trick," I said. "It shows the kind of minds those trying to separate us have. We may have to pass some tests on the way back, but I think there's no doubt that the ones behind these tests were the Dark Powers. If the Olympians test us on the way back, it may be harder to pass the tests, but they won't be so unfair." She nodded. "Yes, I agree. We seem to have survived these attacks, but now we're approaching the moment of truth. Can I live in the Bright Land or not?"

We could see a light at the end of the tunnel, and as we approached it, it grew almost unbearably bright. "Let's go more cautiously from here," said M'pha. "if we can't live in the Bright Land, the light might scar us all over." We came to the mouth of the tunnel and could see that there was a small rocky cave at the end of the Path. We stepped out of the Path and looked out. The scene was familiar in one way, unreal in another. What we could see was the valley where Athens was, surrounded by the mountains I had seen on our way to Athens from the harbor, but there was no sign of human works at all. The valley was as wild and untamed as it must have been when the first inhabitants of Athens came to it.

It was not just the scene which was unfamiliar: the light of the sun which blazed high in the sky made everything look more *real, more there*. I felt that every scene I had seen before was only a pale copy of this *real* landscape. We advanced to the entrance and stood looking out. Suddenly I noticed something about M'pha. Through some chink in the tunnel, a ray of sunlight was shining on her arm. It left no scar and M'pha didn't even seem to notice it. She moved, almost like a sleepwalker, toward the entrance to the cave. "It's so beautiful," she said. "Put your hand out in the light," I said, hoping I was not making a big mistake.

She put her hand out, and her hand, too, seemed to become more vivid, more real. "M'pha, I think you can live here," I said. "Go out slowly, and be prepared to come back to the tunnel if you feel queer." She stepped completely out of the cave, and her whole body seemed to become more *there*. I followed her slowly, hoping that Chryseis had not been mistaken about the powers of my ring, but I could also stand the full glare of the sun, though I did not think it made me more real. "I can live here," said M'pha slowly. Her eyes widened. "And Vicky, so can you."

I shook my head. "The power of the ring protects me in some way. I'm not about to take it off." She looked at me with startled eyes. "How do you know about the ring?" she asked. "Chryseis told me," I said, and all of a sudden, there was Chryseis facing us. "I hoped for this," she said. "I gave all of Alceme's children the treatments when you were too young to remember, but it didn't work with Ducalion, and poor Sarpedon died in the war." I looked at her. "Treatments?" I said. She smiled at me. "If you can live here, but are born in your world, it helps to be exposed to the light second hand, at the hands of someone who is an Olympian. My mother gave me the treatments when I was baby, so the first time I came here through a Path, and met the gryphon, it seemed quite natural for me to live here. Vicky, you said you wouldn't take off the ring, and if that's your decision, that's fine. But if you'd take it off for an instant, I can protect you, and it might help me to learn something.

I took a deep breath. "All right, Chryseis," I said, and took the ring off. Immediately, I felt wonderful, filled with lightness and joy. Chryseis watched me intently and finally said, "You'd better put it on again, Vicky. You haven't had the treatments, and without them you'd have to get accustomed to the True Sun little by little. This knocks in the head a lot of theories people hold about living in the Bright Land. Most people, even Olympians, think that to live here you have to have Olympian blood, but I suspect that Olympian blood is rather rare, if it exists at all, in your time.

"But Chryseis," M'pha said, "I don't have any Olympian blood." Chryseis smiled. "Your grandfather, the Dark Minos, was the son of an Olympian and that's what made him so dangerous when he chose to follow the Dark. I suspect that your other grandfather, Academus, the Councilor, was the son of an Olympian, too, so you fit into the accepted pattern, but Vicky is a puzzle." I reluctantly put on the ring again, but I didn't lose the feeling of lightness and energy I had felt when I had taken it off.

Chryseis reached out her hands and gave us each some small flat cakes. "This is ambrosia," she said. "It helps you to use the energy of the True Sun, and also, more important, to store it until you need to use it. Many of the nymphs and satyrs can live in the Bright Land, but without ambrosia they don't have Olympian powers." The little cakes were good, with a clean fresh taste. I could feel my lightness and joy diminishing, but I had the feeling that I could call it up again when needed.

"You can't stay here long," said Chryseis. "Even M'pha, on this first exposure, can only take a limited time here without getting a sort of sunburn. But you have a problem to face. You now know that you can both live in the Bright Land. What are you going to do about it?"

Chapter Fifteen

"I don't know," said M'pha. "If I'd had any idea that living here could be this wonderful I'd never have asked Telemachus to give it up. Now that I know, I just can't make a decision." Chryseis smiled at her. "You have plenty of time to make up your mind. Incidentally, your visit here has taken years off your age, M'pha, and even a little off yours, Vicky. You have lots of time to make a decision." I stared at her. "I'll look younger?" I asked. Chryseis chuckled. "When I got back from my first trip here, Ariadne told me that my hair had gotten brighter. I'm not sure *your* hair can get any redder, Vicky, but you will look a bit younger and have some extra energy, and I wouldn't be surprised if you could control animals even without your ring. Rings and amulets only focus the power we have inside us."

I said slowly, "So if for some reason I have to give up this ring, I'll still have some powers. That might make it easier for me to give it up if there were a necessity. And you'll get me back to my own time, Chryseis: I don't think any of my powers could do that." M'pha looked at me. "You aren't tempted to become an Olympian?" she asked. "I may be," I said, "but the whole idea is so new to me that I haven't really grasped it. What about you?" She said slowly, "I don't know. Having Chryseis and Ariadne and Dion visiting us when we were growing up gave me some sense of the powers of the Olympians--and their responsibilities. Anyway, Chryseis said I'd have plenty of time to make up my mind."

"You will," said Chryseis, "and it, as you say, involves a lot of responsibilities. I think you should see Telemachus when you get back, and perhaps talk with Odysseus. He had a decision to make: he'll tell you about it because he's really fond of you. But don't necessarily be guided by his decision." M'pha shook her head. "No, this is a decision that can't be made by anyone else. I think we'd better go now. This place is beautiful and so wonderful that it's hard to decide here." Chryseis nodded, "You're right. Go back down the path; there will be some challenges along the way, but these will be Olympian challenges, not ones made by the Dark Powers."

We turned back to the Path and slowly, with many a backward glance, went down it. As we got into the cloudy tunnel and the light behind us faded, M'pha said to me, "Vicky, you're...glowing." I laughed. "You ought to see yourself," I said. "I think you'd be too bright for anyone to look at unless you had the same experience as I did. You can't go on the streets of Athens looking like that. Can you control the glowing? I think the Olympians must be able to do it." She stopped and closed her eyes. Presently the glow faded, and she said, "Yes, you can control it. It's a little like being a tauromath--you reach out and contact--something-- and tell it what to do."

With that as a clue, I was able to dim my glow and we went on down the corridor. Ahead of us we could see the figure of a woman. At first I thought it was Chryseis again, but she was more mature, and her expression was severe. "You helped yourself quite freely to the Path from my temple," she said. "I'm sorry, Lady Athena," I said, "but Chryseis suggested that we take the Path to find--something." Athena gave a noise I would have called a snort if it hadn't come from a goddess. "That girl takes a great deal on herself; but if you came with her permission it's not your fault. I'll speak to that scamp presently." There was affection in her voice and I thought I need have no fear for Chryseis.

She looked at us and said, "What you discovered is that you can both live in Olympus. Someone has to say this sometime, and it might as well be me. We Olympians are few in number and we can always use help from those who can live in Olympus and who follow the Light, not the Dark. Chryseis, Ariadne, and Dionyseus have added immensely to the good we're able to do. We'd like you to join us, M'pha. Your friend is a traveler in time and poses special problems, but she could probably join us, too. Or else--I don't promise anything-- we might be able to give Telemachus power to live in Olympus. He can't survive there now, but certain things can be done. Odysseus already knows that he himself can live there but has chosen not to."

M'pha took a rather shaky breath. "Must I choose now," she asked, "and if I choose to have Telemachus with me, do I have to make the choice to come there before you see if he can?" Athena shook her head. "Neither condition would be fair to you. Take time to make up your mind, and if you choose to have someone with you, we'll find out if that is possible before you make your final decision. One last thing: my niece would be very glad to have you join us, but she didn't want to influence you in any way so I was sent to make this offer. Farewell, M'pha, I hope I see you again." Athena turned and went down the Path in the direction from which we had come.

M'pha turned to me. "I may be wrong, Vicky, but somehow I don't think you would want to join the Olympians." I shook my head. "No," I said, "there are things I have to do back in my own time: I don't really belong here. Parting from you would be even worse this time, but I don't see how we can stay together unless you choose to come to my time." M'pha looked at me. "I wonder if that's possible?" she said, "It's certainly something to keep in mind. Perhaps Chryseis could tell us." We started on the Path again. "Are you sure that was Athena?" I asked. She nodded. "Yes, she looked and acted as I would expect Athena to act, and I don't think that the Dark Powers would dare to disguise themselves as her. If we meet anyone else on the Path we'd better make sure that they're what they appear to be. Look up ahead. Is that...but it can't be."

But it was. M'pha's mother was waiting for us on the Path. She hugged her daughter and me. "It's really me, Phane," she said, "I'm no stranger to the Path anymore. I've been running errands for some of the Olympians, and I got a reward for my labor, an answer to the question I've had ever since your father died, Phane. It's easier to show Vicky than to tell her, and I can do that most effectively if you and she come as pilgrims to Eleusis. You were there once when you were quite young: I'd like you to see it now that you're more mature. Vicky will need to see it, too." She turned to me. "The scene the Dark Powers showed you actually happened, Vicky. It wasn't the whole story, but it did happen". M'pha laughed. "I was indignant at seeing it, but Vicky defended you."

Alceme laughed. "Thank you, Vicky," she said, "Don't take anything the Dark Powers show you at face value and be a little cautious about what the Olympians tell you. I think you've been to the Bright Land and found you can live there?" We nodded. "And you're probably thinking how wonderful it would be to live there forever, but any of us can live there in the long run with all that we truly love. You've been told this, Phane: more than people usually are who are only initiates, but now you have to see it. Come on the next pilgrimage; it won't be too far off. I'll see you there." She hugged us again and went in the direction we were going, but turned to the right where we were always turning to the left to get back to our own world.

"Well, she certainly looked and acted like Alceme," I said. M'pha laughed. "It was mother," she said, "for one thing she called me 'Phane which is an old pet name she had for me. It means 'golden one' and it's what the audience at the Dance used to call her when she was a Leaper." I nodded. "Well, there's no doubt that she has your best interests at heart, and mine, too." Privately I thought that by giving M'pha her old Leaper's nickname, she was saying something about M'pha herself and her own second career as a wife and mother. "Your name has a word for gold in it, doesn't it?" I asked. "Yes, it means 'sea gold'," she said, "but the names of a lot of people connected with the sea have the initial 'M' in them. Minos, for example, means 'seaman's king'."

I sighed. "I wonder what our third test will be. The first two weren't all that bad. All the same, it was a shock to see, crouched in the corridor ahead of us, a figure with an eagle's head with ears, a lion's body and great wings folded at its side. It was a living Gryphon, the kind carved on my ring! A high, remote voice came from it. "You had best touch me so as to see that I am no illusion." We approached a little fearfully and stroked the feathers which covered its head and breast. The smaller ones were soft and springy, but the larger ones could almost have been carved out of gold. The remote voice went on, "I am Gyros, King of the Gryphon Tribe. You have each worn a ring with my picture on it and, on the whole, you've made good use of it. We offer you a bargain. Each of you may call on us for help once, and we will also help you one time if you agree to a request. You, in turn, must promise to fulfill those requests we will make of you, one for each of you and one in which you will have to cooperate. I can tell you nothing more now. Do you wish to make the bargain?"

M'pha and I looked at each other: who could know what the gryphons might demand of us, but their help would be formidable. M'pha had told me enough stories about Chryseis' dealings with the gryphons to assure me of that. "I will," said M'pha, "how about you, Vicky?" I said slowly, "Yes, I think so. Our friend Chryseis has told us about her dealings with you, but how will we know what you want us to do and how can we call on you for help?" The gryphon nodded his massive head. "You will know when we want something of you by the sign or symbol of a gryphon

The Gryphon Seal

given to you. As for calling on us, we will do as we did with Chryseis; each of you take one of my feathers." We did and then the gryphon said, "Put both your hands into and grasp a feather together. Now pull it out." We did and this time the feather split between us, leaving each of us with half. "If you need help, throw the feather into the air, but the feather you each have half of must be put together before you can use it." The gryphon stretched its mighty wings and flew up through the shadowy ceiling, which seemed to part for it.

I sighed. "I'd have liked to ride him like Chryseis on my ring," I said. "Perhaps you will," said M'pha, "but that's not something that you could ask all by itself. We mustn't waste our wishes. Do you see what a terrible responsibility we've taken on? Not only to use our own wishes wisely and agree on a joint wish, but also to do whatever they request of us. Perhaps we shouldn't have been so eager to agree."

I laughed. "Somehow, I think whatever they want us to do will be for our good. We both trust Chryseis, and she trusts them. Besides, what an adventure." M'pha grinned at me. "Yes, of course it is. I don't think either of us could turn it down." It struck me that M'pha had gotten her old expression back, eager and curious. Hoping not to spoil the mood, I said, "Are you going to speak to Telemachus when we get back?" She nodded. "In fact, I may ask you to speak to him first," she said, "but somehow, after the experience of the Bright Land, I can't feel worried. Things will turn out for the best. Isn't that the mouth of the tunnel ahead?"

It was indeed and we stepped out into the little alcove between the statue of Athena and the treasury wall. As we were making our way out of it, a temple official bustled over to us, indignation on his face. But we still glowed faintly with the light of the Bright Land and he stopped and brought his hand up as if to shield his eyes. "Bright Ladies," he said. I smiled at him. "We had Athena's permission to use the Path," I said. "I am sure that you did," he said. "If the Temple can be of any assistance to you, call on me. I am Sosames, one of the priests here." M'pha turned to him. "There is a young man named Telemachus staying with some friends outside of Athens. Can you get him here--about this time tomorrow?" The priest bowed respectfully. "Easily done, Bright Lady," he said. "It would take a brash fool to refuse a request in the name of Athena from us at the temple."

"Well, he's not that," said M'pha, as the man bustled away, "and maybe he'll show what kind of man he is when he comes here. Vicky, will you talk to him first when he comes; sort of break the ground? Then I'll talk to him, and begin to make up my mind." I nodded. "All right," I answered. "What do you want me to tell him?" She shook her head. "Use your own judgment," she said. "I'm too close to the problem to make a judgment."

That didn't help all that much when I met Telemachus the next day. He was a handsome and sturdy lad with some resemblance to his father, from the glimpse I had of Odysseus when he met M'pha the day before. In fact, he was better looking: Odysseus had legs a little too short for the rest of his body;

Telemachus was more evenly proportioned. He looked at me with puzzled eyes. "Here I am, Bright Lady, "he said, "but what does Athena's temple require of me?" I looked at him approvingly. "I'm a friend of Helen, the Queen of Sparta, and her friend, M'pha." Better to put it in that order I thought. "Queen Helen is concerned with the breach between you and M'pha. I have been appointed a sort of ambassador to see if the breach can be healed."

His face flushed and he had what seemed to be a rather self-pitying expression on his face. "The Queen is very kind," he said, "but I don't see how outside interference can help." Because the two of you are behaving like fools, I thought. "On the Path you took from Knossos, M'pha was disappointed in you." I said, ignoring his words. "Disappointed in *me*?" he said. "Yes, in you! When Hermes told you that only one of you could live in the Bright Land, M'pha expected you to say that if both of you could not be together there you would live together in this world, rather than be separated."

His face was filled with honest bewilderment. "But it must be her," he said, "who could live in the Bright Land. She has all kinds of Olympian friends and she always looks as if she never ages even though she was a Leaper in Crete before I was born. My father told me that someday Lady Helen might live in the Bright Land. I have no connection with Olympians except through my father who is a friend of Lady Athena."

"It doesn't work that way," I said. "No matter what connection you have with Olympians, the ability to live in the Bright Land is something born in you: it doesn't depend on your merits or your friends. M'pha's brother found out that he could not live there." His face looked intent. "He hinted at something of the kind when I met him in Crete. Of course if I thought it was I who could live there I'd gladly have given up immortality for her. Even now, even though we quarreled, I'd still give up any hope of immortality for her sake."

"M'pha is sorry for some words she said to you on the Path," I said. "She said you'd never be the man your father is, meaning to hurt because of her disappointment that you didn't make the offer then and there. But Telemachus, do you really want to be like your father?"

Chapter Sixteen

"But my father is a great hero, everyone admires him," he began. "Some people do; others think he's a liar and trickster," I said. "Yes, he was a hero at Troy, but that war is over. Do you want another war where many people are killed and wounded to give you an opportunity to be a hero yourself? What did his absence for ten years after the war mean to your mother? Don't you think you could be a better husband and a better King of Ithaka than he was?" He looked at me with startled eyes. "I sometimes think I could," he said, half to himself. "My father is so clever he doesn't really understand our farmers and fishing folk, and mother was hurt when he didn't come back after the war. I thank the gods that there is no war to call me away from any family I might have, but I think I'd have made more effort to get back than he seems to have done. Some of the things that happened on that journey also hurt my mother; Circe and Calypso, for example. Perhaps I *could* be a better husband and a better king than he was."

"I think M'pha really loves you," I said. "Will the two of you at least talk?" His face lit up. "Gladly, "he said. "Wait here, I'll send her to you," I told him and went to where M'pha was waiting. "You two talk," I said. "He did think you were the one who could live in the Bright Land, and I tried to restore his confidence a bit by running down Odysseus. Make it clear that you only want Odysseus as a friend and father-in-law, and if you can find a few things to say against Odysseus, I think it would help." She grinned. "Odysseus is my friend but I know his faults. Bless you, Vicky. I'll see you back at the ship, or, I'm sure that Cousin Menesthius is probably arranging quarters for us. If you want to go there, just leave a message with the captain."

I left her there and started to walk back to the ship, but I was intercepted by a pleasant looking older man. "Lady Vicky?" he asked. "Your red hair makes you easy to spot. King Menesthius has quarters for you near the palace: in fact, there's an entire wing being prepared for Queen Helen and King Menelaus for their state visit. I am Antithes, a steward of the king. May I show you there and send for your baggage from the ship?" I nodded, "That would be very pleasant, sir. Can someone tell M'pha where I've gone when she comes out of the temple?" He smiled. "Lady M'pha is well known to us here in Athens. I'll leave a trusty servant to give her your message; no need for either of you to make a journey to the port. Rumor has it that you were a Leaper with Lady M'pha. Do you also come from Caria?" "A bit further off," I said, and Antithes did not press the point.

M'pha arrived at our new lodgings very late, with stars in her eyes. "You and Telemachus seem to be reconciled" I said. "Did you and he make love?" Her cheeks reddened. "Not all the way," she said, "but everything up to that point. He's still being noble about not actually having sex until we're married. Actually, I don't see the point, but it's really a way of showing me that he values me, not just lovemaking." I said, "I wouldn't have asked, but I've been told on good authority that if you're not a virgin you can't travel in time. This idea of you coming to my time is very attractive, but I know that Telemachus is more important to you."

She laughed, "Actually I'd like to do both; but you're right, Telemachus is more important. Let's see what happens. Vicky, I can't thank you enough for what you said to Telemachus. He's been in the shadow of his father all these years, and the thought that he might be a better husband and king than Odysseus was is a new and rather stimulating idea to him. If he could find something else he could accomplish which his father hasn't done, I think that the cure would be complete."

"Do you know if Telemachus has still not made love to a woman?" I asked. "Yes, he told me so, and of course, with Odysseus away and the suitors in the house, he didn't dare to fall in love. I think he's the kind of man who wouldn't make love unless he were in love." I laughed. "As opposed to his father," I said. She grinned. "I still have a lot of admiration for Odysseus, but I think he's not the model of a faithful husband. He sent letters from Troy to Telemachus and told him about an affair with a nymph which shocked Telemachus. I think Odysseus forgot how young Telemachus still was at the end of the war and got interested in his experiences and said more than he should have to so young a boy."

"The reason I asked," I said, "was that perhaps Telemachus could come with you to my time." She looked at me. "That would certainly be something Odysseus has never done," she said. "Do you mind if I tell him about you and the possibility of going to your time?" I shook my head. "No, not at all," I said, "but I think we'll have to make that our joint request to the Gryphons. I brought Dorothy with me, but I don't think I could get her back and the two of you, too. We can ask Chryseis."

She nodded. "Right now, Telemachus is talking to his father. He's been avoiding him ever since Odysseus got to Athens. I think that Odysseus is clever enough to see his problem and give him some encouragement to think better of himself. Penelope will be delighted. I wish we could find a man for you, Vicky, but it would have to be someone from your own time, I suppose, since you think that eventually you will go back and stay there. Why should this be our joint wish; I can make it my wish."

I shook my head. "No, I think we'd better keep our individual wishes for emergencies. What if Telemachus got sick, or Dorothy got into some kind of trouble in this time. You've told me enough about Chryseis' adventures to make it clear how useful a wish granted by the gryphon is. Let's go to bed in adjoining beds, M'pha, and you can spend tonight telling me all about Telemachus." She did, but eventually we had to sleep, and if I was a little groggy the next day, M'pha was still bright and eager. Telemachus called at our lodging fairly early, and I saw them go off together with a touch of envy. I had met some good men in Crete, and Steven Banter, Mumford's bear leader, I thought would be an interesting man to get to know better, but would I ever get all starry eyed about any man? I could see myself as a vigorous and independent spinster, making my own way in the world. Perhaps even having lovers, as Lillie did, but not necessarily marrying any of them.

The Gryphon Seal

I chuckled. Aunt Maddie and even Margot would be shocked by such a plan, but what I didn't want to do was to make any man my 'lord and master'.

It was not long after the reconciliation between M'pha and Telemachus that Helen and Menelaus arrived in Athens on their state visit. All day they were kept busy with ceremonial visits, but late the following evening, Helen came to my room. M'pha was, as usual, with Telemachus. Helen hugged me. "Dorothy is tired but the two of you can get together tomorrow. I saw M'pha and Telemachus together at one visit. We couldn't really talk, but they both looked very happy. Tell me what's happened." I told her all about everything that had happened since I had last seen her. She said, "I'm glad you've seen the Bright Land: it gives you an understanding of how things work here, and that will increase when you make the pilgrimage to Eleusis. I'm glad you have the Gryphons on your side, they're really a form the Old Gods take and I think they may be able to do some things that even the Olympians can't do."

"I'm glad M'pha and Telemachus are together again and I hope it lasts." I looked at her, "You think it may not?" She said slowly, "Men and women in love are to be envied, but making that into a marriage requires a lot of hard work. I know M'pha is capable of it; I hope Telemachus is. You see, M'pha had been in the Bright Land: she had a lot of power stored in her body. If she wanted to be reconciled to Telemachus it would be hard for any mortal to resist, but that power will fade, and then the hard work begins. You were probably able to persuade him to meet M'pha so quickly because you had some power from the True Sun even with your brief exposure. I don't entirely trust results brought about by Olympian power."

"Be very careful about telling M'pha about this," I told her. "She's such an honest person that she might feel that somehow she'd made Telemachus love her, and that it wasn't entirely fair. But life is unfair, or seems to be. Many people have fallen in love with you for your beauty, Helen, and that's not entirely fair to those who lack your perfection." She nodded. "Yes, I know. Like anything which gives you power over others, my beauty brings responsibilities as well as rewards. Incidentally, Dorothy is recovering from what M'pha calls being 'Helen struck' Her enthusiasm is for our whole civilization. She talks about being what she calls a 'classical scholar' when she goes back to your time, and she no longer wants to be with me at every moment."

In fact, I found Dorothy pretty well restored to herself when I met her the next day. She was enthusiastic about Helen, but no more enthusiastic than she had been over Christobel Pankhurst, and, as Helen had said, she had a new ambition. "I've heard lectures and read books about how much our time owes to the Hellenes" she told me, "and it really is true. We have such a marvelous opportunity to know what we call the Classical World on this trip. Of course, we can't use it directly; we can't say how Helen really is because we know her. You'd have to give evidence from surviving documents."

"Yes," I said, "for example, in Homer's *Odyssey* there's a section where Telemachus visits Helen and

Meneleus in Sparta. The relations between Helen and Menelaus are rather as we saw them in Sparta--affectionate, even teasing each other." Dorothy looked at me with startled eyes. "Telemachus," she said, "but he's the man M'pha is engaged to--and he's Odysseus' son? We really are living the world Homer described". I nodded. "I've always found that Homer gives a pretty accurate picture of people in this age. How he did it is a different matter: most scholars think that Homer lived about four or five centuries after this time. Perhaps he was a time traveler, too."

Dorothy shook her head. "Sometimes I really can't believe that we've traveled in time. Perhaps I'm in a ward in Hanwell Lunatic Asylum having interesting delusions, but then my father's hard common sense comes to my aid. I am here, so it is possible. I don't have the imagination to have such a fascinating delusion." I laughed. "Somehow, after my first experience, I never doubted that I'd really traveled in time. Training to leap the bull is hard work, and my aching muscles aren't the kind of thing that would come into a delusion. Mr. Evans didn't show me the bull leaping fresco until *after* I came back and I was able to make the dogs obey my will after my second trip. That's why that man tried to kidnap us."

Dorothy shuddered. "That was a really terrifying moment," she said, "and to go from that to seeing Helen for the first time...she really is a wonderful woman, isn't she." I nodded, "Yes, I think she is. She really does have wisdom and compassion as Odysseus thinks, and it is more important than that marvelous beauty. Not that it isn't a pleasure to look at her, see her move, listen to her voice." Dorothy was always prepared to discuss her idol and we did not return to the subject of time travel.

The next time I was alone with Helen we discussed M'pha and Telemachus again. "Perhaps I was too pessimistic, "Helen said. "Young people, and M'pha is still a young person, both mentally and physically, fall in love for all sorts of reasons. M'pha and Telemachus have at least as good a chance as most of them, and if Telemachus gets a little glamour from his father and M'pha gets a little from me, perhaps it helps rather than hurts. For the moment I'm going to assume that things will work out satisfactorily and not worry about it. I'm glad that you, M'pha, Dorothy and Telemachus are all going to Eleusis. Once you're initiates I can talk more freely with you about certain things."

Now I come to a problem in my story, because like all initiates, I took an oath not to reveal what I had seen and done. After long thought, I've decided to write the outline of what we saw and did. Of course, the procession from Athens, the stop on the seashore, and the arrival at Eleusis are well known: it's what happens inside the building at Eleusis that has always been the secret.

When we filed into the space, I was a little disappointed. It was a big room and the ceiling was supported by many pillars so that it was very difficult to see what happened at the center of the room, but I could see well enough to see that the priestess who was standing there was Alceme! I realized that M'pha had not told me this because it was part of the mystery. She spoke in what appeared to be a conversational tone, but here voice could be heard in every part of the room. She began by saying that when her husband had died in an accident she had left home with one overriding question in her mind: would she ever see her husband again? She told a fascinating story of her wanderings: to Athens, to meet Helen at a village where she was held after Theseus kidnapped her, and then Sparta, when Helen was rescued by her brothers.

She then told of the capture of Persephone by Hades, Lord of the Dark Land, who was the jailer of the rebel Titans. She told of Demeter's search for Persephone and that she, herself, had gone down into the Dark Land to see what had happened to Persephone. Demeter was withholding the gift of grain from ordinary mortals in an effort to force the Olympians to rescue her daughter from Hades; but Persephone loved Hades and had eaten a pomegranate grown in the Dark Land which meant she could never return to the Bright Land.

At last a compromise was worked out with the aid of the Gryphons: Persephone would come to our world every spring and summer and spend fall and winter in the Dark Land with Hades, and Demeter would give back grain to mortals in our world. This was especially interesting to me because of the Gryphons and a hint or two from Alceme that the settlement had to be imposed on Demeter against her will. You might have missed these hints if you didn't know Alceme, but to someone who did, the hints were not hard to pick up. In reward for her part in achieving this compromise, the Olympians decided to answer Alceme's question about life after death. These mysteries were the answer to her question.

I looked with renewed respect at M'pha, whose mother had persuaded the Olympians to part with this secret. She told me later that her mother had not revealed, even to her family, the vital part she had played in these events, and resolved if I got a chance, to seek from Alceme more details of this story. Alceme concluded her speech with the words, "Praise to the goddess who restored the grain, but she has done more; she and her daughter give us the gift of hope. Listen to the goddess who returned after leaving the land of the living!"

Alceme vanished, and before us stood a female Olympian with an unfamiliar face: from Alceme's words, it must be Persephone. She glowed with the light of the Bright Land as M'pha had done, and somehow the pillars which crowded the room did not prevent me from seeing her. "I am Persephone, the bride of Hades," she said, "the Queen of the Dark Land."

Chapter Seventeen

Persephone said, "Dark to Dark," and behind her a circle appeared in the air, showing a dark, gloomy landscape with no sun and what little light there was coming from a sunless sky. Wandering through the landscape were many figures, each alone and seeming to ignore the others. My eye caught a figure rolling a heavy stone up a hillside. When he had almost got it to the top it escaped him and rolled down the hill. With an air of tiredness and dejection, he trudged down the hill and began rolling it uphill again. Once more it escaped him and he trudged slowly down the hill. Some figures were not moving: I saw a female figure seemingly trapped up to her waist in a rock; she waved her arms frantically and tried to free herself from the rock which held her fast. I realized that I was seeing all this as if the roof pillars had vanished; somehow the scene showed through the pillars.

Persephone said, " If your deeds are dark, behold your fate." I could see Dorothy's face next to me, pale and anguished. Some people around us fell to their knees. Then the landscape was cleared of figures and Persephone stepped into it. "This could be your fate," Persephone said again, "if your deeds are dark and evil." Then the circle in the air vanished. It had not been there long, but it left my eyes and heart aching. Had I done anything to deserve such a fate? Some of my dealings with Aunt Maddie and Aunt Ceal came into my mind. I thought I had been justified, but had I?

Now servants appeared, and took the boxes of earth and seed grain we had carried with us from Athens. They spread the earth and grain in a semicircle around the area where we had seen the circle in which the Dark land had appeared. Then they stepped back: another brightly glowing figure appeared with a certain resemblance to Persephone, but with a more mature look about her. Persephone was an Olympian girl, this was an Olympian woman. "I am Demeter, who sought my child everywhere, and found her in the Dark Land. Light to Light, if your life is just and merciful" Then behind her the circle reappeared and in it was the Bright Land!"

There were figures in this landscape, too, but they were in couples or groups. Some appeared to be talking, others singing, and some were engaged in some sort of dance. Figures of children in little groups or pairs ran in and out of the more adult looking figures.

I looked into the inhabitants of the Bright Land and I saw a couple strolling together, one a tall slender man with a straight back, talking to a woman with red hair very much like mine, but far more beautiful. "Mama," I whispered, "Papa." This appearance was brief, but it left us all consoled and strengthened. When the circle with the Bright Land vanished, we could see that the little heaps of earth and grain which had been laid down, had sprouted and grown. There were tall spires of grain waving around the edge of the circle. The servants went forward with bronze scythes and cut the grain in silence.

Demeter had not vanished with the circle with the Bright Land. She spoke to us sternly, "The land you have seen is very desirable, but you cannot get there simply by longing for its happiness. You can not get there if your aim is simply to be happy in it. You can only get there by living a life worthy of it, with love for your fellow mortals, treating them with justice and mercy." Demeter stood there, real and solid, and blazing with light. She said, "What you have seen is to give you consolation and hope. Do not presume, but do not despair. The Power that bids you to be just and merciful will be just and merciful to you. Wait in hope; terrible and beautiful things are to come. The Holy One must give birth to the Sacred Child, the Mighty One." Then Demeter vanished, leaving the familiar golden motes in the air.

We stood blinking in the morning light coming in from high windows: the torches that had illuminated the room when we entered were out. M'pha and Telemachus were talking quietly, their heads together. Dorothy turned to me, "We've seen hell and heaven, Vicky: and the words at the end; they must be a prophecy of the birth of Christ, our Lord, from the Blessed Virgin." I looked at her. "You may be right," I said. "My aunt, who brought me up, used to talk a lot about religion, but very little about Christ and his life. Perhaps I'd better get a New Testament when we get back." There was very little doubt in my mind that I would have to go back soon. M'pha no longer needed me now that she had Telemachus and I had a feeling that I might be wanted in my own world. "But is Christ just a super-Olympian?"

"No," came a voice from the air near me. "Wait until the last stragglers go out and I'll take off the veil of Addis. You've been to the Bright Land, Vicky. The Olympians draw their power from the light of that land, but I think the person you're talking about must be the source of that light. He is the True Sun." I looked at her, "But what are the Olympians?"

"They're very temporary inhabitants of the Bright Land," said Alceme's voice, as she appeared from the feet up. Whatever had made her invisible was a sort of cloak or veil: I remembered M'pha telling me stories about the Veil of Addis which gave you invisibility. She looked at me, "I want you to understand, Vicky. Dorothy, here, can believe without understanding, but you need to understand in order to believe. The Bright Land is in the future for us mortals, but it always exists. The Olympians are allowed to live there and use its power to help humans. If they misuse its power, they can lose the Bright Land. I think Aries may be misusing his power, and I used to think Aphrodite was, but I'm no longer so sure of that"

"Then the Olympians are like what we call Angels?" Dorothy asked. "Not quite," said Alceme. "They have human blood, all of them. The Old Gods, who appear as gryphons and other sacred animals like the Phoenix and Pegasus, are perhaps really what you call Angels. At any rate, they are the powers of the world, of earth and air and water and fire. One thing neither the Olympians or the Old Gods can do is bring back the dead, as I discovered when my husband died."

"Our Lord raised a number of people from the dead," said Dorothy, "his friend Lazarus, and a widow's son, and a little girl.." Alceme nodded her head, "That's a very good sign that he is the True Sun, the Lord of

The Gryphon Seal

Life and Death. Chryseis' father used to say that the Olympians did not create the world, nor do they rule it, except in limited ways. Perhaps the one you call 'Our Lord' did create the world and does, in fact, rule it." Dorothy nodded, "Yes, he is the Creator and the Ruler, but he was also born in human form--true God and true man."

Alceme shook her head. "For us this must be far in the future, and all we can do is the best we can with what truth we have now. I said a bit more about my own part in the event that led to the Mysteries at Eleusis than I usually do. I don't like to brag, but I wanted M'pha and the two of you to know the truth. It always sticks in my throat a little to give praise to Demeter in these ceremonies; she was a very reluctant partner in the compromise suggested by the gryphons. It was Zeus himself who decided to grant my request to know what becomes of the dead. We made it into a mystery, partly at Ariadne's suggestion, so people in this age would take it seriously." (And that is why I have recorded so much about Eleusis: the 'people of that age' are now dead and gone to one of the two choices.)

M'pha looked up and saw Alceme. "Mother," she said and flew to her arms. "I think I saw father in the Bright Land," she said. Alceme nodded, "I'm very sure he is there, but I've never seen him; probably when I do, it will be a sign of my own impending death. Vicky, I have an idea you must go back to your own time soon--Dorothy also. Is there anything you want to do before you go?" I nodded and said to M'pha, "Shall we make that request to the gryphons we talked about?" She nodded, "Yes, I've talked about it with Telemachus.

Can we call the gryphons here?" Alceme nodded, "It's a good place to do it, but come back: I want to see some grandchildren from you before I die."

M'pha and I disentangled the split feather halves from our hair where we had been carrying them, and tossed both halves in the air. At once the gryphon we had met on the path appeared, lying down with his paws extended in front of him and his head held high. Even crouched like this, his head was taller than ours. "Lord Gyros," I said, "I would like my friend and her fiancé to be able to visit me in my time. Is that possible?" The gryphon nodded, "It was foreseen that you might ask this of us. Yes, it is possible, but it means that what you ask of us and what we ask of you must be done in your own time. Since M'pha will return to this time, that is not necessarily true for her. Do you agree?" I nodded, "Yes, Lord Gyros. Now that Alceme has told us how you helped bring this consoling mystery to people of this time, I'm even more in awe of you."

The gryphon turned his massive head to Alceme. "Hail, Alceme," he said. "We know that you, more than us or the Olympians were the source of this mystery. Hail, Telemachus. You will have more dealings with us before long." He said to me, "This cannot be done immediately or without a great deal of work. You must go back to your own time and M'pha and Telemachus will join you there in Crete." I nodded, "I was already planning to go to Crete. Dorothy, would you like to go with me?" She was looking at the gryphon with widened eyes: it struck me that she and Telemachus were the only ones who had not had some encounter with these creatures. "Oh, yes," she said, "it would be wonderful."

I turned to the gryphon, "Well, our joint request is granted: do you have anything we can do in return?" The gryphon shook his massive head. "Not quite yet," he said. "Perhaps not even until you are in your own time and M'pha with you. You will know." I nodded, "I'm sure I will," I said. "Alceme, would you like to spend some time with M'pha and your future son-in-law? I can take Dorothy back to Athens and wait there for them at Helen's lodging." She nodded, "That's an excellent idea, Vicky, but would you like to have a few private words with them?" "No," I said, "I'd better get back to Athens and make my farewells to Helen and Menelaus." I turned to the great gryphon, "Do you want anything further of me, Lord Gyros?"

There was almost a laugh in that high remote voice. "I am told that you once expressed a desire to ride on my back. Would you like me to take you to Athena's temple with both of you riding on my back?" I said, "Oh, more than anything else at the moment. If I have to leave this time, what a way to finish my visit!" Dorothy was, I think, a little afraid, but she gamely climbed up behind me and held on to my waist. The gryphon gave a tremendous spring and seemed to fly *through* the roof. "It is better that none of us be seen on this trip," it said, "we are not visible to mortal eyes." I laughed, "Perhaps that's just as well; it was the experience I wanted, not the notoriety." Then I was silent as we flew high over the country between Eleusis and Athens. I had never seen the earth from this angle, but I enjoyed it. There were flying machines in my own day: I resolved to get up in the air in my own time, but this was an experience that could never be duplicated in my own time; the mighty body below me, the wings beating the air, the sense of magic and mystery that the great gryphon carried with him.

We circled the Acropolis and landed, and there stood Chryseis watching us. We might not be visible to mortal eyes, but Chryseis saw us. She grinned at me. "I see I'm not the only one to ride a gryphon. Hail, my Lord Gyros." The high remote voice said, "Hail, Chryseis. Your friend is needed back in her own time soon." Chryseis nodded. "Yes, I've been told. I'll be sorry to lose her; she made things much more exciting. Hello, Dorothy. I'm the more or less notorious Chryseis, and it's nice to meet you." Dorothy, her eyes once more wide, looked at Chryseis with awe. "I thought that surely you were Athena herself," she said. Chryseis chuckled. "Thena is my more or less revered aunt," she said. Turning to me, she went on, "Vicky, I hate to tell you this, but your Aunt Margot is dying: that's why you need to go back. I can bring you back to very much the same time you left. I knew that once I told you, you could not be happy staying in this time."

I took a long shaky breath. "You're right, Chryseis," I said. "No matter how much I love being here with you and the others, I couldn't enjoy it knowing about Aunt Margot. I would like to say goodbye to Helen." Then I saw Helen walking by herself, up the hill. "You've told her, then?" she asked Chryseis. "I'm sorry to see you go, but you don't want to stay, knowing about your aunt. Dorothy, you can stay here a while if you want, and we can get you back somewhere near the time and place that we'll send Vicky." Dorothy shook her head, "I want to go back with Vicky." "Thank you, Dorothy," I said. "Will I ever see either of you again?" I asked Chryseis and Helen. "There are possibilities," said Helen. "I think I'll be able to persuade Menelaus to join me in the Bright Land. He's getting increasingly fond of Telemachus, and if Telemachus joins M'pha in the Bright Land, I think he'll join me. If I'm an Olympian then Chryseis and I could see you again. Not in your time, but--elsewhere." "Then I won't say goodbye, only farewell," I said, embracing them both. On a sudden impulse, I embraced Gyros' mighty head and gave him a kiss on the soft feathers of his face.

Chryseis looked at the gryphon. "You'll follow her down the path, as you followed Alceme, to see that she gets there safely?" The gryphon nodded its mighty head. "The Dark Powers may try to stop her. She deserves my protection on her way back, for her sake and yours." Suddenly a shadowy path appeared before us. I took Dorothy's hand and stepped into it, afraid that if I looked back my resolution would falter. We walked for what seemed like a long way along the Path, and then ahead of us I could see the ordinary light of our own world, our own time. "Go in peace, daughter," said the high remote voice from behind us. Don't look back, even now." It was a disappointment, since I had hoped for one last sight of the great gryphon, but obeying, Dorothy and I stepped off the Path.

"We must be in Hyde Park or Kensington Park somewhere," I began, but just then, something came over a nearby wall, a small black and white bundle.

"If you're going to leap on people like that.." said an educated voice from the other side of the wall, "I'm not going to take you home to my children. Fend for yourself, you little monster." I picked up the rather bedraggled black and white cat, the very one which had helped us escape the loutish man, and said to it, stroking its fur, "You're more than welcome to live with me, puss, but I'm afraid I'll have to put you into a box for the train journey. Dorothy, you'd better go to your father and tell him that I had to go home; that Aunt Margot is sick. We'll meet soon enough in Oxford." We embraced, and I found a hansom cab to take me to the station. As usual, in a transfer between times, I was dressed in appropriate clothing for the time with my money and checks in my handbag. I got the next train to Oxford, and the guard winked at me, "Keep the cat out of sight until the train goes, then you can let her play in your compartment." I did so: even though my garments were less decorated with flounces and furbelows than most women's, I had a few deep pockets sewn into my skirt, and the cat rode in one of them until the ticket taker had come and I was alone in the compartment.

In Oxford I took a cab to the house and found Margot in bed, looking very frail. "Oh, Vicky," she said, "I made everyone, even the doctor, promise not to tell you that I was ill. I didn't want to spoil your time in London."

Chapter Eighteen

"And don't you think it would have spoiled more than my time in London if I'd come back and found you dead?" I said. "I'm told on good authority that you're dying, Margot; but don't worry, I can keep you from dying." I could feel the remaining gryphon feather in my hair; perhaps better to wait until I was alone to use it. She smiled at me sadly, "I'm sure you could: you're such a clever girl, Vicky, but I don't want you to. I've been longing more and more to see Petty, even though it means parting from you."

I sighed, "All right, Margot. I know you've been longing for him and you will meet him and be very happy with him, I know." She smiled. You sound very sure, Vicky. Even the minister doesn't sound that sure. I've left the house and what I have in the bank to you. My annuity dies with me, but if you need to you could rent rooms in the house to female students from Somerville." I nodded, "Thank you, Margot," I said, "I'll always have that to fall back on. I'm certainly not going back to Aunt Maddie. Perhaps Dorothy can get permission to stay with me: I know Jeremiah would gladly consent."

It did not take Margot long to die after that meeting. She had great spirit but her poor body was worn out. I found a New Testament and would read to her as she lay taking deep breaths with a little wheeze at the end. We particularly liked John's Gospel and his Epistles. Paul was a little complicated for us. We tried, but I laughed when we came across the words in Peter's Epistle "His words are hard to understand", referring to Paul. We also read a little in the book of Revelations: one passage reminded me of something that Chryseis had said, "The Lamb is the light of that place."

Dorothy came and stayed with us, which was a great comfort. When Dorothy and I were sitting by her bed Margot often talked of her past and Petty's courtship of her. She lasted a month after I came back, and died peacefully. I wired Uncle 'Vestor, who had come several times from London during Margot's last illness, and thankfully let him take charge of the funeral arrangements, only insisting that some of our favorite passages from John's Gospel should be read along with the usual readings.

One thing that made me laugh ruefully was a letter from Aunt Maddie, 'Now that your unfortunate association with Mrs. Pettigrew is over, I might have asked you to return to us, but I can never forgive you for sending Roberta to America with *that* woman.' I had brief messages of sympathy from Robin and Lillie, but it was evident that their travels in America were absorbing most of their attention. A passage in Lillie's letter made me laugh: "If you run across the king, please thank him again for me. His patronage at that special performance has made a success of this whole American tour." I thought I was not too likely to run into King Edward (Wrongly, as it turned out).

Jeremiah was a staunch pillar at the funeral, and after the visitors had gone he took us into Uncle Petty's study. "Perhaps you'd better tell Miss Vicky what happened before you came here," he said to Dorothy. She said, somewhat defiantly, "We attended a meeting at the House of Commons on votes for women: Mrs.

Pankhurst, Christobel and I and some others. The men were so stupid. One of them made a speech, saying that if men came canvassing for women's votes it would lead to all sorts of immorality! Mrs. Pankhurst found that too much and we stormed out of the Visitor's Gallery and tried to have a meeting on the street, but the police kept on chivvying us and eventually some of us were arrested."

"I came down and paid a small fine to get Dot freed. Since I was her father she didn't have to give consent. Mrs. P. and Christbel refused to have their fines paid," said Jeremiah, "even though a number of people offered. They preferred to martyr themselves by serving their sentence. It certainly got a lot of public attention, but I think Dot is a little young to spend time in prison. I know you don't agree with me, Dot, but Mrs. P. did; but the fact that she was arrested got her sent down from Somerville."

Dorothy said, "They don't call it that for women, but I've been suspended for this term, and I'm not sure that I ever want to go back!" Jeremiah nodded, "I think there are some universities, especially in Scotland, that take women scholars a little more seriously. I'm looking into it, but Dorothy is at a loose end for this term and she's got this bee in her bonnet about studying classics. I've been checking, and it's difficult, but not impossible to visit Crete and Athens. I have plenty of connections in the wool trade and I've found a boat going to Crete in about ten days. I'd like well to take you there and I think it would be good for both of you. Will you come, Vicky?"

I couldn't refuse this act of kindness, so I put my affairs into the hands of Mr. Teddings at the bank, put Mrs. MacDonald and Mrs. Fuller on maintenance wages to look after the house and got together what clothing and other possessions I could manage. "Is it still hot in Crete?" I asked Uncle Arthur. He said, "Hot, but not as hot as it is in high summer. Duncan MacKenzie is still at the site, and he'll show you around. He'll arrange lodgings for you and the Kings and send you on to Athens when you're ready to go. No, nonsense child, he'll be happy to do it: he likes you."

One thing I hated to leave behind was the black and white cat which I had somewhat disrespectfully named "Gyros". Neither Mrs. MacDonald nor Mrs. Fuller were cat people, so I finally decided to take Gyros with me: boats were more accommodating than railroads to having your pets with you. So on a fine morning only ten days after the funeral, we all set off.

But one thing happened before that: I wanted to have a look at a flying machine, as I promised myself I would after my flight on the gryphon's back. So Dorothy and I took London Transport to Hendon Airport. We were examining the planes and hoping to see one take off when we encountered two men in flying caps and goggles. They stared at us and took off their caps. One of them was Michael Rese and the other was Stephen Harter. Both were dressed informally and Mr. Rese looked far less formidable than he had at Oxford. "Why, it's Miss Marsden, the 'votes for women' lady. I put Christabel Pankhurst on your trail; hope you don't mind," said Michael Rese. "Not at all," I replied. "She introduced me to my

The Gryphon Seal

friend, Dorothy King. She's a real 'votes for women' woman. She's just lately been arrested for a protest at the House of Commons," I said. He turned to Dorothy. "I've heard about that, Miss King. Shame the way the police treated you. Christabel and her mother are still in prison, aren't they?"

Dorothy nodded, "I would have been there, too, but my father paid my fine. I've been sent down from Somerville for a term." He shook his head. "Bad form, not supporting women who are trying to improve women's lot. Are you two ladies interested in flying?" I smiled at him, "I am but Dorothy is still a little dubious." He turned to Stephen Harter. "Look here, Harter, why don't you keep Miss King company while I take Miss Marsden up. We'll have plenty of chances to fly." Stephen Harter gave me his cap and goggles and before I had a chance to get scared I was in the front cockpit of a biplane taxiing down the runway.

The plane's engine raced furiously, shaking the whole plane. We raced down the runway, then all of a sudden the banging of our wheels on the ground ceased and we were flying. The noise from the engine was almost overwhelming. "Been flying before? Michael shouted. "Not in one of these," I shouted back, "it certainly is noisy." He nodded, "Must have been up in a balloon; far less noisy, but this goes a lot faster and is far more controllable, you can land where you started."

He was silent for a while as I peered over the edge of the cockpit, enjoying seeing the more familiar landscape of England, as I had seen similar views of Athens from the Gryphon's back. This flight was longer, too, but at last we turned back and landed with only a small bump when our wheels hit the ground. Michael got out, then came and helped me out of the cockpit. "Thank you, it was marvelous," I said. "How much does a machine like this cost?" He laughed, "We call them 'kites' sometimes, but they're expensive kites. I couldn't afford one and I doubt you could, but you can join a flying club and rent a plane when you need it. You have spirit: I like that. If you'd like to be the first woman member of a flying club, I'll do my best to see you're accepted".

I shook my head, "Dorothy and I are going on a trip. Perhaps when we get back I'll take you up on that. I suppose I'd need instruction?" He nodded, "I'm a qualified instructor," He said. "These machines are going to be used in the next war, which I think will take place in five or ten years. I'll possibly be too old to fly in battle, but I can instruct younger men. By the way, Mumford was sent down permanently, but I managed to find Harter a scholarship. He's a good man and if we do go to war, I think he'll volunteer for the Flying Corps or whatever they'll call it."

Moving toward us was a little group of official looking men and at the head of them was King Edward! "Well flown," he said to Michael. "This young lady has courage. Good Heavens, it's Miss Marsden. How d'ye do?" I dropped a courtsey. "I'm pretty well, your majesty. My Aunt Margot just died, but Mr. King is taking his daughter and me to Greece." He nodded, "Good man, King. Do you think he'd be offended if I put him on the next honor's list? He deserves it". I smiled at the King. "He'd complain a bit, but secretly I think he'd be pleased if it came from you, sir."

He nodded, "Drop by our embassy in Athens while you're there; it takes a bit of time to work these things." He turned to Michael, "Your face looks familiar, young man" Michael laughed, "I'm Michael Rese, a don at Oxford, your majesty. We've met at some Oxford functions, sir. Flying is my secret vice." King Edward smiled at him. "Very good secret vice to have, Mr. Rese. I'd like to try flying but my advisors won't let me. Have to do the best I can with fast cars." On an impulse, I said, "I have a message for you from Mrs. Langtry. She says to thank you for the command performance." I saw a few faces in the group of officials freeze: evidently Lillie was disapproved of by some , and (as if I cared) I had probably done my reputation no good by conveying the message.

"Alexis and I were happy to do it," the King said. "Alexis likes Lillie. If you write to her, give her my love." The group moved off and Michael looked at me with some astonishment. "So you know the Jersey Lily," he said. "You keep surprising me. When you get back from Greece would you like to have tea somewhere, or drop into a pub for a drink?" I laughed. "I'd like that, but you mustn't confuse me with Lillie; I'm not as adventurous in certain ways as she is." He smiled. "The thought never crossed my mind, but I like you and I'd like to get to know you better."

"All right," I said, "you can take me to a pub when we get back." Dorothy and Steven Harter came up just then and both looked a little startled by my words.

"Sir, Miss King is very interested in classical history and civilization," Steven said, "but she's been suspended from Somerville and may not want to go back there." Michael nodded, "Plenty of good classicists outside of Oxford. Some excellent people at Edinborough, for example. Come and see me when you get back from Greece. Miss Marsden can be your chaperone." I laughed. "My friends call me Vicky," I told him. He grinned, "Miss Vicky, then: don't want to run before we can walk. Harter, you can help me check out the plane and tie it down. Have fun in Greece, ladies."

As we went back to London, Dorothy asked me, "Are you interested in Steven Harter, Vicky; because if you are..." I shook my head. "Actually, I find Michael Rese far more interesting, but I'm certainly not romantic about either of them." Not yet, I said to myself. I could imagine developing that kind of interest in Michael. It would be an interesting life being the wife of an Oxford don and I didn't think that Michael would play the "Lord and Master" over me.

It seemed almost instantly that we were on the ship for Crete. I hardly had a chance to get used to the idea of being in Crete in my own time before we were moored off Canea; our next stop would by Rhythemnon and finally Candia, which the Greeks were beginning to call Iraklion. Jeremiah told us, "I have an introduction to a Greek politician here; quite an important man in his own way. Elephtherius Venizelos is his name. Would the two of you like to meet him?" We assented enthusiastically and were conveyed by carriage to a very simple house where we met Venizelos. He was a middle aged man in a white jacket and trousers and a plain tie at his throat. I had noticed that men either wore western clothing with heavy coats and vests

The Gryphon Seal

(or at least vests) or else a costume which seemed Turkish to me, with baggy pants and a shirt and jacket, generally black. Some of them wore a Turkish fez; others had handkerchiefs wrapped around their heads, like pirates.

Jeremiah introduced us to Mr. Venizelos, "My daughter, Dorothy, and her friend, Miss Victoria Marsden. They are even keener on freedom for Greece and Crete than I am." Mr. Venizelos smiled. "I am very pleased to meet you all. I'm really more comfortable in French, the language of diplomacy, but if you forgive my mistakes, I can make out in English. What do you young ladies know of Greece?" "I'm an enthusiast for Crete, especially its early history as revealed by Arthur Evans' excavations," I said. "My friend, Dorothy, is an enthusiast for Helen of Sparta, and we're looking forward to seeing Athens."

He chuckled, "I know Arthur Evans very well. Perhaps in some ways the early history of Crete is the happiest. I'm interested in your calling Helen "Helen of Sparta' rather than 'Helen of Troy'. My family is originally from Sparta, but I was born here on Crete, and I often have work to do in Athens, so your favorite places are mine, too. Where else would you like to visit?" I told him, "Delphi, of course, and I'd love to visit Patmos. I'm an enthusiast for St. John the Evangelist." He smiled, "We often call him St. John the Theologian here in Greece. The taste and knowledge of your two young charges is indeed impressive, Mr. King. Your interests in Greece...?" Jeremiah laughed, "I'm no classical scholar, but I very much approve of your struggle to free yourselves from Turkey."

Venizelos shook his head, "We are not entirely free. Theoretically we are still an independent part of the Ottoman Empire with Prince George of Greece as our viceroy. Sooner or later we hope for 'enosis': union with Greece, but there are many difficulties in the way. You are an English Lord?" Jeremiah shook his head. "Just a retired business man who still likes to keep an occasional iron in the fire. My own excuse for this trip is to see about importing some of your wool and bringing English woolen goods for your people to buy: not that wool is a very good fabric for this climate: I envy you your white suit."

Venizelos laughed. "On formal occasions I, too, must dress in wool, but for informal occasions, as I hope this is, I value my white cotton suit. White is much the best to wear here in the summer but people rarely wear it. One lady I know who often dresses in white is Miss Boyd, the American archeologist." I looked at him. "She's an actual archeologist like Mr. Evans?" He nodded, "She is indeed. She has a Masters degree from Smith College in the United States, and her work is supported by American scholarships and grants. Mr. Evans and his colleagues have given her a great deal of support and help, but her excavations at Gournia are entirely under her direction. I don't know if she is in Crete now or at the American School of Classical Studies in Athens." I nodded, "I'll find out from someone I know at the excavations at N'sos." He laughed, "You pronounce that like the Cretans do. Are you familiar with modern Greek?"

"No," I said, "My aunt who died not long ago gave me a pretty good grounding in Classical Greek, but the modern language is somewhat different." He said, "There are differences, yes, but to a large extent in pronunciation and the use of some terms which are used in ancient Greek for a different purpose. Wine, for example, is not 'oinos' but 'krasi'." I nodded, "Doesn't that mean 'mixture' in classical Greek?" We continued our talk about language and customs until he glanced at his watch. "I am sorry to cut this conversation short, but I must go now and do something illegal."

Chapter Nineteen

He laughed at our startled expressions. "I am chairing a meeting on freedom for Crete and union with Greece. According to the Turks, such meetings are illegal and the Allied Forces who are here to protect us from the Turks also regard them as illegal. But Crete must be entirely free and union with Greece is our best hope of not being snapped up by some other power and losing our freedom again. Let me give you a little present before you go, Miss Marsden. It is a book by a man whom I think is one of our best poets, C.P. Cavaffi. Since you do not have to pronounce the words, your classical Greek will help you to read it, but I fear there are many modern expressions which make it a little hard for students of classical Greek to understand. I said sincerely, "I'll value it as a memorial of this meeting, sir, and I'll certainly try to read it." He turned to Dorothy and Jeremiah. "I am sorry that I have nothing to offer you, but this is my ancestral home and I hope to improve it some day to come back to, but for the moment I live very simply with a few books to keep me company.

"Don't worry. sir," said Jeremiah, "This meeting has been quite memorable. Dot and I don't need any mementos of it to remember it. If the services of a retired English business man can be of any help, don't hesitate to call on me. Dorothy wants to study classics; you may find her in Greece again. Is there an English School of Classical Studies?" Venizelos laughed. "Yes, but you English call it simply 'The English School'. I hope to meet all of you again."

The Gryphon Seal

On our way back to our boat, I said, "You know, we were treating Mr. Venizelos very much as we treated the King when we met him." Jeremiah nodded, "Oh, aye, he's quite a great man in his way. He'll make a stir before he's done, but he doesn't want to be a king, only the elected representative of his people. Greeks like freedom, even from kings." I nodded, "Yes, you're right. Do you know that his first name means 'freedom' in Greek? From what he said, his name must start with what looks like an English 'B'. Yes, here it is written in the book."

After a brief stop at Rythemnon, where I noticed the prayer towers of the Muslims, we finally anchored in the harbor of Candia (or Iraklion). We were met by Duncan MacKenzie, who told us, "I've got lodgings for you in town. If you were here next year, I'd be able to offer you rooms at our new building near Knossos. Mr. Evans will use it when he's here, but honored guests can use it when he isn't. I've got you rooms in a hotel called the King Minos; the proprietor is a Greek-American who returned to Greece so you'll be able to communicate with him." I asked him, "You speak modern Greek, don't you, Mr. MacKenzie? I'd like a little help with a book someone gave me." He looked at the book. "Well, I'll try to be of some help. I speak Demotiki--the language of the ordinary people. Cavaffi's poems are somewhere between that and the language of the upper classes: that's called 'katerevousa', the 'pure' language and is closer to classical Greek. I'm afraid this is a little high-flown for me or for Nick, the proprietor of the hotel."

Iraklion, as I decided to call it (rather than Candia), was to the east of where Amnissos, the port of ancient Crete had been. It was a rather primitive city, with many unpaved streets and many buildings which recalled the Turkish occupation. Nick had tried to bring his hotel up to American standards, but he was frank about its shortcomings. "There are faucets and even bathtubs, but we only have running water sometimes. One of my employees has to pump water to the tank on the roof, and since I can only afford young boys as helpers it doesn't always get done. The good thing is that the water tank heats up in the sun, and if you choose your time of day for a bath, you can actually get hot water." I laughed, "The accommodations on the ship were not all that good, and at least your hotel doesn't rock as our little ship did."

"Are you glad you came back here from America?" He nodded, "Yes, on the whole I am. Don't get me wrong; the U.S. is a great country, and I made my money in it so I could afford to build this place, but Greeks always miss Greece and try to get back here for visits or to retire. You know 'nostalgia' is a Greek word." I nodded, "Yes, it means something like 'longing for the land' doesn't it? I'm trying to learn some modern Greek." His face lit up, "You just do that," he said. "A returned immigrant like me gets criticized if our Greek isn't perfect, but an obvious English lady like you will get a lot of credit for even trying to speak a few words of Greek. The word 'efcharisto' means 'thank you'; remember 'F. Harry Stow' except that the 'H' in "Harry" is more like the 'ch' in German 'ach'. 'Parakalo' is 'thank you', 'ne' is 'yes' and 'ochi' is

The Gryphon Seal

'no'--the same 'ch' as in 'efcharisto'. 'Where is' is 'pou eyna' and 'poso costyzee' is 'how much' if you want to buy anything. That should be enough to see you through for a while."

Dorothy was tired after our journey and hadn't quite got her land-legs back, so I said, "Don't worry; I'll just wander around the neighborhood." When I got to the door of the hotel, I saw a carriage standing there, and on sudden impulse I climbed into it and said, "N'sos parakalo." The driver looked at me. "To Archeological topos?" he asked. "Ne," I said. He started a stream of Greek which was incomprehensible to me, and I lifted my hands. "Parakalo," I said, "I've used almost all the modern Greek I know." He smiled and said, "You are one of the English ladies staying with Nikos. I speak a little English, you speak a little Greek: we get along."

We drove for what seemed a long time, passing through a massive gate at the edge of the city and going through farmland: lots of olive trees and what I thought was tobacco. I had never taken this route to N'sos, but we passed some familiar hills and I saw ahead of me the ruins of the city I had lived in on my visits to ancient Greece. There was a sort of guard post at the edge of the ruins and my driver spoke in Greek to the gray-blue uniformed man at the guard post. He returned and said, "You can go in and look but none of the English archeologists are here now." Thanking him, I said, "I know Mr. Evans in England and Duncan MacKenzie, who may be somewhere about."

He grinned, "Kyrie Evans--a great man, but Kyrie Duncan is a good friend to all of the Greeks here. I will see if I can find him. Go on in: no one will disturb you." I passed the guard post and tried to orient myself on the site. The regular entrance must be to my left. I could scramble over the ruins to get there directly, but I decided to go around to the entrance and try to figure out where I was. There were some column bases in the entrance hall and the remains of a fresco with a bull on my right. Going up the partially excavated steps, I came out on the central court. There was what looked like the remains of the Room of the Path and I walked over to it. From its shadowy interior two figures stepped out--M'pha and Telemachus!

"We managed to get here," said M'pha. "From all the ruins, I suppose this must be your time." I hugged her and Telemachus. "Yes," I said, "It's a little sad, isn't it, to see it in ruins, but learned men are excavating and learning about the times we lived in. You two look rather spectacular." They were both clothed in modern dress. M'pla's dress was quite a bit more elegant than mine, and Telemachus wore a well cut gray suit. "It's hot in these clothes," said Telemachus. "Do people really wear all this stuff?" "I'm afraid they do," I said. "I've seen pictures of my friend Mr. Evans working in the ruins while he was dressed very much as you are now. If M'pha and I went around in Dancer's kilts here, we'd probably be arrested for 'indecent exposure'."

M'pha laughed, "I've been on some trading ventures where Mother and I had to envelope ourselves in clothes which fit the conventions of the people we were trading with and Telemachus is a priest and a prince, so he's had to wear some far from comfortable ceremonial robes. We can stand it. I take it that we are now speaking the local language, as you did when you came to our time."

"Well," I said, "You're speaking the language of my homeland, England. Whether you can speak the local language is another question." It was soon to be answered; a Greek workman came up and spoke to us in Greek. Telemachus answered him in what seemed to be the same language. The workman gave a respectful nod and went off. "I wish I could speak modern Greek as well as you seem to," I said. Telemachus shook his head. "I'm not conscious of it being any different from what I'd speak in Athens or Sparta. Both Phane and I have native languages; Ithacan for me and Carian for her. Both are based on Cretan, so it's not too surprising that we switch from one language to another more or less without thinking. We address people who speak to us in their own language in that language.

Two things that Telemachus said interested me. He was calling M'pha by the pet name her mother had given her, 'Phane'. It argued a certain amount of affection for her. The other thing was this matter of switching from one language to another. Out loud I said, "I wonder if I'll ever make the transition from one language to another that automatically. I'm working on ancient Greek and now I'm trying to learn modern Greek, but I never had to worry much about pronunciation when I was learning ancient Greek with Aunt Margot, and I find a lot of the pronunciation and some of the words have changed."

M'pha laughed, "It seems strange to hear the language you've grown up speaking called ancient Greek, and I suppose you'd call our times ancient, too; ancient Greece, ancient Athens and so on. That, together with the ruins, makes me feel a little queer, but I'm glad we're together again, if only for a time. You notice that a lot of these supernatural things seem to go in threes. I wonder when we'll be asked to do together the thing the Gryphons demanded of us in return for the wishes they gave us..." A familiar high, remote voice said, "The time is now. There is a man in this time who is important to the future of this land. Vicky has already met him." The voice came from what looked like a painting of a gryphon on the wall of the room of the Path, but the eyes, especially, did not look painted: they seemed to see us.

I gasped, "You must mean Elephtherias Venizelos. My friends and I were saying that he seemed an important man." The high remote voice continued, "He is proving a thorn in the side of the Turkish authorities and to the allied powers here from your land and other neighboring countries. It has been agreed, not quite by the top authorities, but by zealous subordinates, that he will be arrested and killed, seemingly by accident. The thing we ask of you is to prevent this. You have a few days and he will be coming to the modern city near here for meetings before they act, which will give them an excuse to arrest him. We know you can do it, if you both try very hard, with the aid of this young man here."

"Of course, we'll do our utmost," I said. "I liked Mr. Venizelos and he was kind to me, but even if we get to him, will he believe us?" The remote voice said, "In one way or another, you must do it." Then the figure on the wall became a painted gryphon again.

We looked at each other. "I suppose that we're not together just to remember old times," said M'pha. "Well, the first time we met, you and I were learning to leap the bull, and the second time we met, you came with me onto the Path. I suppose that saving the life of a man from assassination isn't much more difficult." I laughed. "Well, it's a different sort of problem. You've told Telemachus about what we found on the Path?" This time it was Telemachus who replied, "Yes, we had a long talk about it. I don't want Phane to give up the possibility of being an Olympian for me, so if it can be managed, I suppose I'll go to the Bright Land with her. Neither Meneleus nor myself really feel comfortable about the idea of becoming Olympians, but at least we'll have each other for company. Helen and Phane will make wonderful goddesses, and we'll support them in any way we can. Thank you for your words when we met in Athens, Vicky. Now that I've traveled in time, I've done something my father never did." He grinned and said, "Even if he does, in some way travel in time, on this occasion I'll be the first to do it."

I felt better about Telemachus: that old resentment against his father which had kept him unsure of himself seemed to be gone. I wondered if this was the reason the gryphons had brought him and M'pha to this time. M'pha said, "I want to use my own wish with the gryphons to make sure that he can live in the Bright Land, but he's resisting the idea."

Telemachus shook his head. "You may need that wish," he said, "besides, the Olympians want you to join them; let's see what that can do before perhaps wasting Phane's wish." M'pha laughed, "There speaks the son of the crafty Odysseus," she said. Telemachus grinned at her. "I'm no longer rejecting my inheritance from him, now, since it doesn't seem to leave me in the shade. I can now ask myself what my father would do in a given situation and choose whether I'd do the same thing. Right now my practical instincts tell me that we'd better find a place to stay and get some information about where the man we're supposed to protect will be."

"You can come with me to my hotel, the place I lodge with Dorothy and her father. I think you can tell them that by some accident you've lost your luggage." Telemachus nodded, "And I think we'd better be Greek immigrants to some country safely far away to conceal our lack of knowledge about present day Greece." "It can't be England," I said thoughtfully, "because Jeremiah, Dorothy's father, would know too much about England, and it can't be America, because the proprietor of our hotel is a returned immigrant from America. How about Australia? I think there are some immigrants from Greece there, and I don't think anyone we're likely to meet knows much about it."

Telemachus laughed. "Sounds like a a good idea. Now tell me everything you know about Australia." It didn't take long, but Telemachus nodded as I finished. "I think that will be enough with a little cleverness on our part. Where did we meet you?" I said, "It had better be in London. I've told M'pha enough about my life there for you to make a plausible story of a visit there. I suppose we'd better get back to the hotel."

Just then we heard a noise at the entrance to the Room of the Path and Duncan MacKenzie came in.

The Gryphon Seal

"I'm sorry there was no one to meet you, Miss Victoiria. Some Greek friends of mine were having a wedding and it took a while to track me down there." I took his outstretched hand and said, "Don't worry about it Mr. MacKenzie. These are some friends of mine whom I met in London. They're Greek by background but have lived in Australia most of their lives." Mr. MacKenzie shook hands with both of them. "I'm Telemachus Ithakis and this is my wife, Phane," said Telemachus. MacKenzie looked at M'pha admiringly and said, "Her ancestors were certainly from Crete; like a lot of Cretans she has a face that might almost have come from one of our frescoes. By your name, you must be from Ithaca. Welcome back to your ancestral home. I wish you could see the frescoes of Gryphon in this room, but the originals are being worked on and we haven't put reproductions on the wall yet." He gestured to the wall, and where we had seen the painted Gryphon, there was only a blank wall!

Chapter Twenty

"I can imagine it, "said Telemachus. "You're painting reproductions of the frescoes here?" Duncan's face lit up. "Yes, we're trying to restore some parts of the palace to look as much as possible like the original palace. Let me show you around." Turning to me, he said. "I've sent your carriage back to the hotel with a message that I'm showing you the palace; then he'll come back for you. Don't worry about paying him: he's the tame carriage driver for the hotel. Nikos will pay him and put it on your bill. Some people might be shocked at you coming out here by yourself, but Mr. Evans and I know you pretty well and we know you wouldn't worry about it, but no use causing a scandal. Why even Miss Boyd, when she was traveling around Crete with a muleteer had him bring his mother along as a chaperone. She's about as independent as you are, Miss Victoria, but as I say, no use giving the Mrs. Grundys something to gossip about."

I laughed, "Thank you, Mr. MacKenzie. I've heard about Miss Boyd: is she in Crete now?" He shook his head and said, "She's in Athens now, riding her bicycle all over the city as she always does. I'm sure you'll get to meet her there. Mr. Evans has a lot of admiration for her work in excavating Gournia; says it's work that any archeologist could be proud of." M'pha looked at him and said, "Gournia? Was there a palace there, or only a town?" MacKenzie's eyes lit with enthusiasm. "You must be taking an interest in Cretan archeology, Mrs. Ithakis. Yes, Gournia was just a village, but that's why

Miss Boyd's excavation there supplemented our work here. Let me show you what we've done."

He showed us all over the site and we could see how the restoration really did capture something like the look N'sos had had. There were the familiar red or black pillars, tapering toward the bottom, the stairs not too much damaged and frescoes which looked familiar in some of the palace rooms. "We think that this block of rooms were the queen's quarters and those down the little corridor were the king's." I nodded and said, "Yes, black pillars with red capitals and bases in one room and red pillars with black capitals and bases in the other." He agreed, "Yes, but unfortunately we can't carry out that scheme anywhere else: red and black pillars seem to be distributed all over the palace. We found some rather lovely frescoes in what we call the queen's room and a remnant in the king's room of what looks like the chair in the throne room where I met you, except that it was wood, not carved in stone." I nodded: those high backed chairs were the captain's chairs on the Cretan ships but only Minos could be seated on one on land. "Surely the room you met us in is a little small for a throne room," I said. He nodded and said, "You're quite right, Miss Victoria, but since we found that stone throne in it, people have begun calling it 'the throne room'. I think, myself, that perhaps some kind of ceremonies were carried out there." I murmured, "You may be right, Mr. MacKenzie."

He said, "No need to give me that name; Duncan will do fine." I laughed, "Then you must call me Vicky, as my friends do." He said, "Well, perhaps, Miss Vicky. Mr. Evans will be delighted when I write that I've shown you over Knossos. He says you have a very good instinct for what makes sense in the context of ancient Crete. We're calling it the Minoan period now, you know. He lowered his voice, "Please come when you can; I'll tell the guards to let you in any time. Knossos by moonlight is still quite a sight to see, even in ruins, and the same applies to your Australian friends who seem very knowledgeable. I haven't tried speaking Greek to them, but one of my workman said Mr. Ithakis spoke beautiful Greek, real Katherevousa. My own modern Greek is mostly Demotiki, the language of the working people." I said, "Thank you, Duncan. I'll take all advantage of your invitation I can: I may bring my friend, Dorothy. The carriage driver said that Mr. Evans was a great man, but you are a great friend."

He laughed, "Mr. Evans takes a more formal approach to our workmen than I do. I like to go to their celebrations and I'm fond of a drink called raki which they like. Mr. Evans sometimes says I'm a little too fond of it--and them." I shook my head, "I think you and Mr. Evans are quite clever in the way you deal with them. He's the rather remote authority figure and you're their friend and companion. Have your excavation crew been with you for a long time?" He laughed, "Yes, many of them have been with us since we began excavating here. When he's annoyed with them for some reason, Mr. Evans says they've been with us too long, but I think he's as fond of them as I am."

It was late in the afternoon when we took the carriage back to the hotel. Nick accepted our story about their luggage being lost and said he could loan Telemachus a few things if Dorothy and I could help M'pha. He gave them the best room in the hotel, the Bridal Suite, which Jeremiah had rejected as too expensive. "Very nice people, your Australian-Greek friends," he said. "They speak a beautiful Greek, a little old fashioned sometimes. Their parents must have been people of importance. Probably they left Greece because of the Turkish occupation: that's why I left."

M'pha came to my room to borrow a few things and I said, "You and Telemachus still haven't...?" She shook her head. "We're officially married, but waiting until this is over to make love. My brother Ducalion and his wife, Acama, were in the same situation: they were officially married, but waited until after the last Dance to make love. When this adventure is over, we'll console ourselves by making love and trying to be good rulers, but perhaps we'll never equal our parents." I said, a little tentatively, "Telemachus calls you Phane, as your mother does, but you use his full name." She laughed, "He hates being 'called out of his name'. In particular, he very much dislikes 'Telly' which might be the natural shortening of his name." She blushed, "Of course I do have some pet names for him, but they're not for saying in public. How about you, Vicky: any men in sight?" I said, "Well, perhaps one. He's a teacher at Oxford like my Uncle Petty." It occurred to me to wonder if Uncle Pettygrew really liked having his name shortened to "Petty"; but I had the feeling that he'd accept anything from Margot, as I would, even if we didn't like some things she did. He would put up with it because he loved her.

I introduced Telemachus and M'pha , whom I had to remember to call Phane to Jeremiah and Dorothy. Jeremiah was quite impressed with them. "This Mr. Ithikis has quite an aristocratic air, even a sort of royal one, and his wife is charming. Except for Mr. Venizelos, they're the most impressive people I've met here. I'd like to visit Australia some day, but it's a long trip and perhaps I'm getting a little old for long trips like that. They have good sheep and good wool in Australia, but Mr. Ithikis didn't have any details. He does know his sheep and something about wool, but isn't certain about what their production is. Well, he's a gentleman, not a businessman." When I reported this conversation to Telemachus, he laughed. "A king in Ithika is hardly more than the largest landowner on the island and a war leader. I could probably give him details about sheep and wool on Ithika in my own time, but I certainly don't know much about Australian production."

Dorothy was used to me having somewhat exotic friends from my London days, and she accepted them at face value, only remarking how much Phane looked like that friend of Helen's, M'pha. I realized that she had been too taken up with Helen to really look at anyone else, and I decided to let sleeping dogs lie: not involve Dorothy too much in this visit of M'pla's. Actually, Dorothy and her father were enjoying each other's company, spending a lot of time shopping in Iraklion while I tried to renew my acquaintance with this modern island of Crete. I often blessed Miss Boyd, who had set the example of an independent woman with her own interests in the ancient culture of Greece.

Actually, even by English standards, I was fairly well chaperoned by my friends, Mr. and Mrs. Ithikis and of course their knowledge of Greek made things much easier. Telemachus told me, "I've gotten some Athenian newspapers, and the educated language, katheravousa, is not too far from the Greek I know, and if I'm speaking to those who speak Demotiki, I try to be more simple and informal as I would with laborers on Ithika. Whatever brought us here seems to fill in any gaps: everyone can pretty well comprehend me, and I often get compliments on how well I speak."

M'pha and I were even closer than we had been, but there was a certain air of saying goodbye in our relationship; even if we had lived in the same time, her marriage would have taken her away from me to some extent. She and Telemachus spoke to Greeks they judged trustworthy about Mr. Venizelos and we thought we could locate him before the planned arrest. Duncan was delighted when we went to the site. He said we had a real instinct about life in ancient Crete and we were a great help to him in his work. Actually, it was Duncan who gave us our first real news of Mr. Venizelos. He approached me one day and said, "Your friends have been making some quiet inquiries about Eleutheris Venizelos. People have asked me about you three, and I told them you loved Crete and could be trusted. Mr. Venizelos will be at a meeting of his supporters tomorrow night. It's supposed to be a secret meeting, but I wonder if too many people know about it. I'll give you directions to the house if you want to meet him."

Telemachus borrowed a carriage from one of his Greek friends and we took it to the meeting the next night. We left it in charge of a small boy and walked a few streets to the meeting. The doorkeeper hesitated a little before letting us in. We were taken to a back room where Mr. Venizelos was working on some papers.

"Sir," said Telemachus, "we walked here from a few streets away. There are Turkish soldiers hidden nearby and we have information that you will be arrested and 'accidentally' killed. Please, you must leave this house now." "You are friends of Miss Victoria, and by your speech an educated man. I could ask why I should trust you, but somehow I do. If we go out the back way, I think we can avoid he troops. I've sometimes wondered if I should allow myself to be arrested, to cause protests, but my plan was to be arrested by the allied forces. I wouldn't trust the Turks not to do as you say, kill me and pretend it was an accident."

Venizelos seemed to know the neighborhood and we worked our way by quiet streets to where the boy was holding our horses. "Let's go at normal speed, so as not to arouse suspicion," I said. Just then I heard shouts and sounds of running boots. "Whip them up, Telemachus," I said. "I think someone back there knows Mr. Venizelos has escaped. Take the road for N'sos: we know it well now and we can hide in the ruins."

Venizelos looked at us with keen eyes. "It would be a good idea to stay away from places where other people might be arrested if they find me, but all three of you are risking your lives. Why?" Telemachus said, "The future of Crete and Greece is important to all of

The Gryphon Seal

us, for different reasons. Don't worry about us: we have ways of protecting ourselves, especially at N'sos." We careened through the town and out the deserted streets to N'sos. The gatekeeper recognized us and I told him "You haven't seen us," as we abandoned the carriage and ran into the ruins. He nodded, slapped the horses with a stick and sent them off down the road.

"I think we should go to the Room of the Path," I said. Venizelos eyed me. "You three are very familiar with these ruins," he said. "Like most Greeks, I have two religions, Christianity and a sort of half belief in the old Gods, and when things like this happen, I wonder." We went into the Room of the Path and for a while things were quiet, but then there was shouting at the guard post and the sound of shots. Some voices could be heard and Venizelos said quietly, "They are saying in Turkish to hunt through all the ruins."

I sighed, "I was afraid of this, M'pha. I think it's time for you two to go back. I think the Path will open for us." And, indeed, the shadowy tunnel appeared at the bottom of a set of stairs. Venizelos did not lose his calm, "The archeologists say that pit there is for ritual washing." "Not quite," I said. "Come with us, sir, and we'll be undisturbed while they search the ruins."

We walked down the shadowy tunnel a little and I embraced M'pha. "We'll see each other again some day," I said. "The showing at Eleusis tells us that." I hugged Telemachus. "Take care of her," I told him. Venizelos shook hands with both of them and we watched them walk away down the tunnel.

"May I ask where they are going?" he asked. "Back to their own time," I said. "The man is Telemachus, son of Odysseus. The girl is a sister of the last Minos of Crete. She was a bull leaper." He shook his head, "To be rescued by people from our past makes me proud, but also humble. But you are English?" I nodded, "Yes, but I've been to the past along just such a tunnel as this; but my time for adventuring in the past is over and I must do some things in this time now." He nodded, "And so must I. How long do we need to hide here?" Suddenly a great gryphon was beside us. "No need to hide," said the high remote voice. "I think I can make your enemies run away. You and your friends have done well, daughter. And you, whose name means 'freedom', lead your people into full freedom and try not to hate the Turks too much," he said to Venizelos.

Venizelos nodded, "I will try, but it will be difficult." We emerged from the entrance to the Path, the gryphon going before us. When we came out of the tunnel, there were shouts of panic and the sound of running boots. "I do not think there will be any Turks here for a long time," said the gryphon, and vanished.

"Nevertheless, I had better make my way across country to a safe place," said Venizelos. "I might be in Athens soon: I hope to meet you there." He gave me a formal Greek hug, touching one cheek to one of mine and then his other cheek to my other cheek. Then he vanished into the darkness. When I got back to the hotel, I told Jeremiah, Dorothy and Nick that my friends had a chance to leave the island by a boat going in their direction. "I think they'll probably visit Ithika," I said. Jeremiah said, "I'll miss those two, and I noticed you were particularly fond of the wife. Quite a pair. Well, if it's all right with you, I've made a reservation on a boat for Athens. I'd like to visit some of the smaller islands but I'm afraid it's Athens, then home for us."

Nick was sorry to see us go. "I'm not sure I can make a go of this place with the Turks still here. I may look for a place in Athens, myself. Do you know that a bunch of drunken Turks broke into the archeological site at Knossos and did some damage? Something scared them, though, and you can't get a Turkish soldier, or even a Turkish officer, anywhere near Knossos. By the way, I won't charge for your friends brief visit here. It was a pleasure to have them. I wonder if they ever recovered their baggage?" I smiled, "I think they have everything they need now. They're fairly wealthy and so am I. I'll gladly pay for their stay." He laughed, "No, no, my pleasure, and don't go telling people that you're fairly wealthy. With that and your beautiful hair, you'd have a line of suitors stretching from here to Knossos."

Duncan was also indignant about the Turkish raid on N'sos. "We've located the ringleaders," he said, "and they're being sent back to Turkey in disgrace. Every so often the Turks forget that they no longer rule this island, and every time they alienate the Allied Powers, like the time the British Counsel was killed. Mr. Evans says that eventually the Turks will have to leave Crete altogether; but then, he got in trouble in Serbia as a young man, agitating against Austrian rule there. I've nothing against Johny Turk in his own country and some of the people who worked with Dr. Schlieman liked the ordinary Turks very much, but their rulers are tyrants and they don't belong in Crete."

I said slowly "Well, perhaps neither do I," Duncan shook his head, "You'll always be welcome here, Miss Vicky, not only at the site but also amid the ordinary people of Crete. I hear some rumors that Eleutharios Venizelos was helped by three strangers to escape from being arrested, and perhaps worse. I suspect you know something about that." I smiled, "These things get exaggerated," but for the rest of my stay on Crete, I was as popular among the Cretans as I had been as a Leaper in Minoan times.

Chapter Twenty-one

When we got to Athens (I suspect one step ahead of the authorities, who were looking for a girl with red hair who had helped Venizelos escape), Jeremiah was at first busy with meeting Greeks and foreign businessmen, as he said, 'keeping an iron in the fire' by making contacts for the businesses he still owned but did not actively manage. Dorothy and I spent most of our time investigating Athens, along with a guide, Kosta, who had been hired to show us around. Kosta was a student at the University of Athens who got some money for his studies by doing guiding. Sometimes he had classes or examinations which he could not neglect, and then Dorothy and I spent most of the time shopping in the markets near the base of the Acropolis.

The Acropolis, of course, even in ruins, was much more impressive than it had been on our trip to ancient Greece. The massive Parthanon, even though it had been partly destroyed in a battle between Turks and Venetians, was indeed a beautiful building, much more impressive in real life than in photographs we had seen. There was even a photograph of the Parthanon hung in a corner of my aunt's house. The Erectheon with its porch roof supported by carved maidens, caryatids, was also a beautiful building . We knew what the caryatids were: they were women who had carried baskets of earth and seed on our visit to Eleuthsis, and baskets of grain from there in other ceremonies.There were all sorts of ruins surrounded by modern buildings in Athens, especially central Athens which occupied the site of the old city. A fair number of Greeks had come back to Greece from Turkey, though not the flood which was to come after the war with the exchange of populations. Some of the bigger streets were impressively wide, but most of Athens had narrow, twisting streets, with some of the more remote ones little more than unpaved tracks. We stayed at the Grande Bretagne, the best hotel in town; quite equal to Browne's in London, but I saw little hotels run be Greeks in the side streets. I thought then that if I ever got back to Athens, one of them would be my choice; and so it has proved to be.

The museums were filled with beautiful and interesting things, but since I've visited modern Athens many times it's hard to remember what was there on my first visit. I know I always liked more or less complete statues rather than those which had been too severely damaged and bronze rather than marble statues. Dorothy was very fond of the things made of gold, especially the jewelry. She was now getting more elegant in her dress, and began wearing corsets with stays—pieces of whalebone to 'firm' the figure, which I swore I would never do.

One day, Jeremiah came back to the hotel looking a little bothered. "I've been to the British Consulate," he said, "and the King of the Hellenes would like to meet me. I got some rather broad hints that some kind of honor is being given to me, perhaps a knighthood. I'm not sure I like that," he said.

"I'm sorry, Jeremiah," I said. "When we ran into King Edward, he asked me if you'd like to be on the Honors list. I told him you would, if it was an expression of how he felt about you. If I was wrong,

The Gryphon Seal

I'm sorry." "Well, I have mixed feelings about it. Gilbert Chesterton's friend Hilaire Belloc once wrote a poem in which he scoffs at honors. The man who is supposed to be writing the poem, mentions that he still has 'my father's grandfather's father's name unspoiled, untitled, even spelt the same'. I like that point of view, but it would be good for business to be Sir Jeremiah and it might help Dot to make a marriage that would otherwise be beyond her reach. I suppose I'll accept it: it would be awkward to refuse it here in a foreign country. You were right, Miss Vicky, as an expression of confidence from King Edward, I do value it. They asked for me and my daughter to come to the palace, but I'm sure I could get an invitation for you."

I shook my head, "I wouldn't mind encountering King George in informal circumstances, as I've twice met our own King, but I'm not one for formal occasions. For one thing, I don't wear a corset with stays; I'd practically be a pariah. Men can't always tell, but women can. Luckily, I'm fairly trim and in good condition and my own waist is fairly slender, so, as I said, men can't usually tell." Jeremiah laughed, "Some people might say it was a mad excuse to miss a formal reception with the King, but I'm on your side, Miss Vicky. I'll be respectful to the King, but if he asks my opinion of anything, he's going to get it."

When Dorothy and Jeremiah returned from the reception, Dorothy was in ecstasies about it, but Jeremiah was somewhat grimly amused. "When the King deigned to converse with me, he asked where else I had been in Greece. I told him, Crete, and mentioned my admiration for Mr. Venizelos. His Majesty was not pleased. Prince George, the Viceroy of Crete, is his second son and apparently Mr. Venizelos had been giving him a hard time about standing up for the native Cretans more, and not deferring so much to the Turkish interests. It makes me admire Mr. Venizelos even more, and I don't think the King was at all pleased with me. If the honor he was handing on to me from King Edward was within his control, I don't think I would have gotten it."

I smiled at him, "I didn't want to prejudice you, but Kosta, our guide, is quite a republican. He disapproves of King George on principle and says he's too fond of the Germans which may cause Greece some trouble some day. So, you did get an honor from King Edward?" He laughed, "You can call me Sir Jeremiah if you like. I'm not sure if Dot is 'Lady Dorothy' or just 'the right honorable Miss King'. She'd be pleased to be Lady Dorothy, I think, which is one reason I went along with this."

"I shall certainly call you Sir Jeremiah on formal occasions," I said, "and call Dorothy Lady Dorothy if she likes, but our neighbor in Oxford, Lady Tenshaw, once told me I wasn't all that impressed with titles, and I think she was right." He chuckled, "I'm not all that impressed by them, myself," he said. "You've a good hard head under that red hair, Miss Vicky. Jeremiah is good enough for me, whether the occasion is formal or informal." I smiled at him, "And Vicky is good enough for me, Jeremiah." He shook his head, "Well, perhaps only on informal occasions. I wouldn't be surprised if some of the people I meet think I'm traveling with my daughter and my mistress, and calling you Miss Vicky helps to correct that."

I grinned at him, "Given other circumstances, Jeremiah...." He shook his head reprovingly, "Not something to joke about, Vicky. People might confuse you with your friend, Lillie Langtry." I shrugged. "They could do worse," I said. "I don't really know what I want to be, but I'd like to have some kind of title that indicates what I have accomplished. There are women physicians now, but it will be a long time before they admit women barristers, and Oxford won't even give women degrees." He nodded, "I think Dot, when she gets tired of social popularity may go back to her idea of being a classics scholar. You don't see yourself in that role?"

I frowned thoughtfully, "I don't know, Jeremiah. I'd like something a little more active and a little more concerned with people, not just ideas. I do admire Mr. Evans and this Miss Boyd I've heard about. Archeology seems to involve physical activity, not just teaching and scholarship." As a matter of fact, it was not long before I met Miss Boyd. Dorothy was drawn into the social whirl of Athens since she went to the reception and I liked wandering about Athens, trying my ancient Greek and my growing stock of modern Greek on friendly passers by. Since I dressed much more simply than most women, I was often mistaken for a school girl, and Greeks are very fond of children. I was walking down Adrianou Street in the district at the foot of the Acropolis when I saw a young woman on an ordinary English bicycle stop at a shop and go in.

She wasn't in there long and I approached her when she came out.

"Excuse me, but would you be Miss Harriet Boyd?" I asked. "Duncan MacKenzie in Crete says Miss Boyd goes around Athens on her bicycle and yours is almost the only one I've seen." She gave me a keen glance, "Yes, I'm Harriet Boyd. How do you happen to know Duncan Mackenzie?" I told her, "I was living in Oxford with my aunt, who's dead now, and I did some work for Arthur Evans, cataloging his collection. I'm Victoria Marsden."

She held out her hand, "Dr. Evans is a wonderful man. He's been a great help to me in my own researches, and Duncan is a nice fellow. Look, there's a little outdoor cafe a little way off where women can be served without too many problems. Come and have something with me, I'd like to talk to you." When we were settled at a table under an arbor, she said, "The best way to get a glass of water is to order a coffee. They always serve you a big glass of cold water with it." I smiled, "Yes, I know, but I like the coffee, too." An older man with an apron came to the table and showing off a bit I told him "Dio cafedes, parakalo--metrio." He nodded and went into the kitchen.

Miss Boyd blinked at me. "My, you are an experienced traveler," she said. "What are you doing in Athens?" I told her, "I'm here with a friend and her father. She's at Somerville but got suspended for taking part in some suffragette activities and was arrested with some of the Pankhurst family, so her father invited us to Crete and Athens as a sort of consolation prize." Miss Boyd nodded with a serious expression, "Good for

The Gryphon Seal

her and good for him for supporting her. I very much approve of votes for women, but I think my present job is to establish a female presence in archeology. Dr. Evans has made it a lot easier, bless him. I think most men are a little afraid of female competition for jobs, but a man like Dr. Evans is quite sure of himself and has no fear of competition." I nodded, "I think you're right." The one man who had been really unpleasant to me was Mumford, who had no reason to be sure of his intellectual or other capabilities. The men I liked were Mr. Evans, Michael Rese and Duncan MacKenzie, all of them at the peak of their professions with plenty of friends and respect from their collegues, secure in themselves.

"Are you interested in archeology, or did you just happen to do these jobs for Mr. Evans?" Miss Boyd asked. "I'm not sure what I want to do, but Crete and Greece are certainly fascinating places," I said. The man with the apron came back with our coffee and water, and I said, " Efcharisto, Kyrie, poso costisi?" He shook his head, "No charge. Welcome to Greece." When he went off, I looked at Miss Boyd. "Wasn't that kind of him," I said. Miss Boyd nodded, "It's what they call 'philotimo'; what we might call 'love of honor' and most Greeks are xenophiles--lovers of foreigners. But you do the 'Alice' thing quite well." I laughed, "A friend compared me to Lewis Carroll's Alice, and if it means being open and friendly and courteous to people you meet, why not?" We went on to talk about a great many subjects. Harriet, as I was soon calling her, was a very intelligent woman, with opinions on a great many subjects, some of which I agreed with and some not, but like Mr. Chesterton she liked a good argument. "Look," she said, "I have a number of errands to run today, but I'll give you my address; I'm staying with a nice old lady near the American school. I'll be working on reports tomorrow, but come in any time and we'll have a meal or at least some coffee. I don't have any counterparts to my work in archeology in England and I'd certainly like to encourage you to follow my example, but you seem interested in many things."

"I'm more or less on my own today," I said. "If you're going back to your lodging, I could accompany you so I'll know where you live." We walked along, Harriet wheeling her bike, but on our way we encountered a young Greek boy, who approached us with hope in his eyes. "My sister," he said, "she is very ill. Could you foreign ladies help her?" I said at once, "Of course," and Harriet came along a little more reluctantly. This, of course, could be a ploy to rob or otherwise injure us, but I thought the worry in the boy's eyes was genuine. We were led to a small shack, leaning against a ruined wall. Inside were two more children, a toddler and an older girl with a pale face, lying listlessly on a small bed.

The girl looked very much as Robin had when Aunt Maddie sent me to her house to read the bible to them, and it was evident, that like Robin, she had for one reason or another taken over the management of the house. "My mother is dead," said the boy. "We very much depend on my sister, Alika, for everything."

The girl, Alika, looked at us and tried to rise. "Pericles," she said, "I didn't try to teach you English so you could bother foreigners on the street. I'll be better presently." Harriet, now reassured about our reason for being there, examined her gently. "I did a nursing course at one time," she said. "My mother always thought that I should have something to fall back on if archeology didn't work out. Alika, I have some medicine here I got for a colleague. It will help you to feel better, but you must rest; let your brother help you with your chores." The boy nodded, "I will do everything." I pressed some money into his hand. "Buy what you need with this," I said. He looked at me, "We are not beggars," he said with dignity. "I only thought that foreign ladies would know what to do." I looked into his eyes. "Please take it ," I said. "Your sister reminds me of a good friend of mine who isn't with me any more. You can pay me back later. I'll come here again."

Pride struggled with need in his face. "Yes, I will pay it back,' he said, "with interest" As Harriet and I left the house she said, "I think it's her heart. She's probably overstrained it taking care of her brothers. I think the father may be one of the workmen who are restoring the Acropolis. They're brought here from the islands and the law is, that if they put up a house overnight, no one can evict them. It looked like that kind of construction." I nodded, "And he has to work and depends on Alika to take care of the family. Well, it's better than other situations I've seen. They could have been in worse condition; the house is clean and the boys look well cared for. My friend, whom Alika reminds me of, had a dead father and a drunken mother. I was able to help her with her life; perhaps I can do something for Alika." Harriet shook her head, "I think her heart is very weak; I'm not sure she'll make it."

That evening I strode up and down the room. Finally I took the Gryphon's feather from my hair and threw it in the air. Gyros, the black and white cat who had been with me on the ship and in the hotels I had stayed at (though I had concealed his presence from the more senior staff at the Grand Bretagne) came out from under the bed. He jumped and caught it in mid air. At first I was angry at him for interfering, but then something about the pose of his body reminded me of the way that the gryphon had looked. The high remote voice sounded in my ear, "You have a request for us?" "The girl I met today--will she die?" The cat's head nodded, "There is nothing in this time which can save her." I looked at the cat, "Can you save her?" The small head nodded. "If you request it," the voice said, "but she is nothing to you."

I shook my head. "She came across my path," I said, "like that man who was beaten and robbed and the Samaritan looked after him." There seemed to be approval in that remote voice as it said, "You have grown, daughter. Do you wish to see our help in the recovery?" "No, if you say it will be done, I know it will be."

"Then I will give you the task that you promised to do in return," said the voice. "Take training as a healer in this age. You will not regret it." I looked at him. "You mean as a doctor or a nurse?" The voice said, "That is up to you, daughter, but I think I know what you will choose. This does not mean you must be only a healer. Choose what path in life you wish, but be a healer as well." I nodded. I might start out being trained as a nurse; that would involve no battles, and if I liked being a nurse, I might very well take on the battle of becoming a woman doctor. Anyone with any sense appreciated a good doctor and I would have respect from those I respected. "All right" I said. "Will I see you again?"

"Perhaps," said the voice, "and perhaps your friends, who are or will be Olympians, but for the time being, go back to your everyday life. Your aunt is dead; your other friends do not need you now, though they may in the future. Find a little happiness for yourself." Then, the cat, along with the feather, vanished. Well, I suppose losing a cat in a foreign country is not all that unusual, but I hated to be compelled to put on a show of concern, perhaps offer a reward.

The next morning, after breakfasting alone, I went out to the front steps of the hotel. A small figure dodged under the arm of the protective doorman and came to me. I waved the doorman away. "I have your money," Pericles said. "My sister made a recovery last night about seven: she is as fit as she ever was." He grinned, "She has even taken on a new member of the family; a black and white cat that came to our door. The strange thing is that she hadn't taken the medicine that your friend left. Here it is." He handed me a small packet and the money I had given him. "My father got a bonus at work." His face fell, "Only I don't have anything to pay your interest."

I looked at him. "If you pay back the money the next day, you don't have to pay any interest," I improvised. "Take care of the cat for me instead: I used to have a black and white cat." He nodded and turned to go. "Come see me again" I said. "We have a guide, a university student. Even if you can't afford to go to university, he could train you as a guide" (At my expense, I decided.) "That would be wonderful," he said. "Aliki said, if I learned English there would be many opportunities." He ran off and I called after him, "Tell Alika I'll drop by soon."

"Miss Vicky," came a familiar voice from behind me. It was Michael Rese, looking dapper and distinguished in a light weight suit. "I'm here for a conference. I hope you won't think that I'm pursuing you!" I laughed, "It would be a bit flattering if you were." "Would you like to take a walk through Athens and perhaps have lunch at a taverna I know?" he asked.

"I'd like that," I said. There were many ways of being happy; travel, friendship, and perhaps something more with Michael. I didn't regret the Bright Land (for now). I still had the Gryphon Seal Ring, not for travelling in time, but for other uses. There were many enjoyable things to do in this time and place.

About The Author

Richard Purtill is Professor Emeritus of Philosophy at Western Washington University, and the author of twenty published books, including The Kaphtu Trilogy, The Parallel Man, Murdercon, and J.R.R. Tolkien: Myth, Morality, and Religion. He often visits Greece and lived several years in England. His stories have been published in The Magazine of Fantasy and Science Fiction, Marion Zimmer Bradleys' Fantasy Magazine, Alfred Hitchcock's Mystery Magazine, and Isaac Asimov's Science Fiction Magazine.

He is a popular presenter at conferences and conventions, and has been guest of honor at Mythcon in San Diego. He is a member of Science Fiction and Fantasy Writers of America, The Author's Guild, and The National Writers' Union. For more information, see his official website at http://www.alivingdog.com

Printed in the United States
35418LVS00001BB/205-213